FINDING HER
FAMILY'S LOVE

By Kayla Kensington

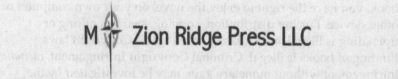

M ✝ Zion Ridge Press LLC

Mt Zion Ridge Press LLC
295 Gum Springs Rd, NW
Georgetown, TN 37366

https://www.mtzionridgepress.com

ISBN 13: 978-1-955838-14-6

Published in the United States of America
Publication Date: February 1, 2022

Editor: Sara Foust
Editor-In-Chief: Michelle Levigne
Executive Editor: Tamera Lynn Kraft

Cover art design by Tamera Lynn Kraft
Cover Art Copyright by Mt Zion Ridge Press LLC © 2021

Dedication

To my husband John, for his love and encouragement, not enough words exist for me to express my gratefulness and love.

Chapter One

Heart thrumming, Kendra McFarland stood outside the farmhouse and waited for the rest of her life to begin.

"We're here, little one." She gave her still-flat belly a pat. Kendra couldn't wait to tell her mother-in-law the news about the baby. She imagined the woman's delight would equal hers. Mrs. McFarland deserved to be the first one to hear about Kendra's pregnancy and warmly welcome her and the baby into the family.

Soon, she'd meet her Shallow Stream, Illinois, relatives. Instead of the McFarlands' vehicles crackling across the gravel driveway, only the chirps of robins greeted Kendra. Her mother-in-law, Mrs. Meryl McFarland, had scheduled the extended family to gather at 3p.m., exactly when Kendra arrived for this first-time meet up. Where was everybody? No cars lined Hickory Road, a remote street that her GPS had difficulty locating.

Her stomach fluttered. Perhaps, the family would stop by later that Sunday afternoon, clutching steaming chicken casseroles and chocolate chip cookies warm from the oven. Her mouth watered. Even more, she craved the idea of sharing a meal. Family. She rolled that delicious word around her tongue.

Strolling along the cobblestone path, crimson rose bushes edged both sides of the curved pathway. Rosebuds leaked their sweet scent, and, overhead, the leaves rustled. A hint of a summer storm sliced through the 90-degree air, but Kendra still shivered. On the freshly painted front porch, a new-looking mat proclaimed, "Welcome."

She smiled at the simple word.

Before she reached the doorbell, a man in his thirties, clutching a water bottle, flung open the front door. Placing the bottle on the front porch's wicker chair, he bent to tighten his athletic shoe's laces. Then he looked up and gazed right at her. His gray-blue eyes sparkled under his thick brows. Her heart quickened. His stance reminded her of the way her late husband stood. She bit her lip at the memory of her David, gone from her life only two months ago.

The guy on the wraparound porch stood taller. Wind ruffled his dark, wavy hair, but he didn't bother to smooth it back. Unlike her late husband, he didn't shout or scowl.

"Hi, I'm Kendra." She took a deep breath and held out her shaking hand to accompany her trembling voice. "Uh, David's wife. I'm happy to be able to meet the whole family today. I...I guess I should've said I'm David's widow." She'd never get used to that term, especially being widowed at age thirty.

He shook her hand. Shock flitted across his face, followed by a smile. "Hey, I'm Pierce, David's cousin. Thought I'd never meet you." He leaned forward. "This is a wonderful surprise, you dropping by today. Though I'm very sorry for your loss."

"Thanks." Surprise? She didn't "drop by" either. The promised welcome party would occur that afternoon. Unless she messed something up again. Wouldn't that be fitting? She swallowed the tears that now always bubbled close to the surface. "Your aunt invited me, 3p.m. today. We've scheduled this."

How could this miscommunication have happened? She fumbled in her purse. Locating her phone, she checked her calendar, which confirmed her statement.

Color rose over Pierce's cheekbones. He cleared his throat. "You must be mistaken. My aunt never mentioned you'd visit, and that's not like her."

She thumbed to the email thread. When she found it, she held it up for him to read.

Folding his arms across his chest, he skimmed the emails, eyebrows raised. He seemed to chew his next words as the lines on his forehead deepened.

"We were surprised none of our family received a wedding invite," he said.

What in the world was he talking about? Kendra shook her head. "I thought...David said...He said none of you wanted to attend."

"Kind of difficult to attend when we weren't invited." Hurt punctuated each word. "Then, there was the funeral."

"No funeral," she said quickly. She hoped that fact would push away the sadness that filled his eyes. "Until I found the letter from David, I didn't know how to locate his family. His letter included the home address. At first, I only had your aunt's email."

This hadn't been how she imagined meeting the McFarland family. No open arms drew her into warm embraces. No "we're thrilled to meet you." Pierce studied her. Kendra guessed he worked as a lawyer. He seemed quite adept at cross-examinations.

"What letter?" he asked.

She put her hand to her mouth, and she wished she could take back her words. When would she learn to stop and think before she spoke? Again, she fumbled in her oversized purse until she found the envelope.

"Read this."

"Dear Kendra," he began, reading aloud.

"You can skip the first three paragraphs." That part of the letter professed all her late husband's love she yearned for but never experienced. She shuddered. Kendra couldn't bear to hear the lying words read aloud. "Go to the last paragraph, please."

He nodded and continued to read. "If anything happens to me while I'm overseas, I want to tell you I don't believe in banks or life insurance." Pausing, he glanced up at her. "Sounds like David. Always suspicious." He returned to the letter. "There's money, my money, hidden away at my childhood home. Please ask my mom or my cousin Pierce. You can trust him, and money doesn't interest him. Here's the address."

"So *that's* why you're here?" His eyes blazed. "Money. You want money." He thrust the letter back to her as though he couldn't touch it another moment. "I can't believe this."

"No, that's not why I'm here. I wanted to meet the family," she said. Especially now that she had no family.

"After you collected the money, you mean." His voice sounded as sharp as the stormy summer wind that tugged at her French braid.

Her cheeks burned. "It's...it's my money." When her late husband died, everything in her life crumbled to the point that, if she didn't maintain her positive attitude, she'd expect a hurricane to wipe everything else away. After all the heartache she'd been through, she at least deserved that, didn't she? What he left for her, what he wanted her to have to start life anew. Besides, she had someone else to think about now. Her hand rested on her belly.

The wind whipped around her and tugged at her blouse, making her shiver. Dark clouds rolled across the sky. "Is your aunt here? May I please see her?" Nearby, thunder boomed. She jumped. A moment later, lightning crackled.

He lowered his voice. "She's resting. I don't want to disturb her."

"I'd like to wait," she said, when he didn't offer that option.

The sky opened. In a staccato burst, rain pelted. She huddled under the covered porch. Would he really make her stand outside until his aunt woke up?

His jaw clenched. "You must understand. Aunt Meryl lost her only son."

She lifted her chin and straightened closer to his height. "And I lost my husband." He appeared to forget that fact. Each day, as new life bloomed inside her, she remembered.

"Yes, and I am sorry. You arriving here to demand some kind of hidden treasure ranks as the last thing my aunts needs now."

Her heart thudded. She knew how bad this sounded. She took a deep breath and prayed she'd say the right thing. "I didn't plan to tell anyone about the letter…at least not yet. David wanted me to have that money." She shivered as raindrops pelted.

He motioned her forward inside the house, shutting the oak door behind her.

She peered around the foyer decorated with an oriental-style runner that brightened the swept hallway. In the silence, the grandfather clock tick-tocked.

Years ago, David had walked these floors, took his first baby-stutter steps here, and, later, he had sprinted and slid across the slick hardwood like slipping across an ice-skating rink. Kendra held back a sigh.

His hand resting on the doorknob, Pierce paused. "David was a good man."

She raised her eyebrows. When she dated David, she had believed that. He brought her bouquets of peach carnations with love letters tucked inside. When he told her he loved her, he gazed into her eyes, and the rest of Milwaukee faded away. His sincere-sounding words melted her heart like that gooey chocolate candy he always gave her. She couldn't disclose to the McFarland family the sad truth about David, not now, maybe not ever. Pulling on her summer sweater, she wrapped it around her like a cocoon.

The hardwood living room floor that glimmered under her sandals creaked with each step. The midnight-blue drapes covered the picture window and eclipsed the storm. No breeze snuck through the windows. She fisted her hands to keep from drawing the drapes or flicking on light switches. This darkness would be like living submerged underwater. The storm made it worse, but still. Was that what David had experienced living here?

Motioning her to sit on the loveseat, a questioning look flitted across Pierce's face. "When my aunt said David had married, it shocked us."

Her stomach flipped. What? "Why?"

"He vowed he'd never marry."

She swallowed hard. What a strange thing for him to say. When David proposed on their second date, it was as unexpected as an August snowstorm. Pierce settled in the high-backed chair nearest her, his long legs sprawled. Without him saying a word, his distrust caused the room to close in on her.

Her frizzed curls fell, wet against her neck. She couldn't let this confusion continue. "He married me, and this was the date and time his

4

mom invited me to visit." Should she refer to Mrs. McFarland as "mom?" She'd only known her through a handful of emails signed with the woman's initials, MM, never her name. No "love," "warmly," or even "fondly" had appeared.

"I'm certain my aunt didn't know you'd arrive here today seeking money." He leaned forward. "She won't take this well, especially as she fights her grief."

She worried a loose string on her skirt's seam. After everything that had happened with her late husband, she had hoped that his family would be happy to meet her and welcome her with smiles. The familiar twist of her stomach caused her to cover her mouth and jump from the love seat. *Oh no, not now.*

"Bathroom?" she mumbled.

Trying to stop the tsunami of nausea, she held her breath.

"Follow me." He rushed her down the hallway.

The toilet, which would've required her lifting the lid, wasn't an option with both hands cupped over her mouth. With less than a second to spare, she made it to the sink, then slammed the door closed with her heel. Luckily, she hadn't vomited on him.

The cool water she splashed on her cheeks and ran over her wrists stilled her stomach's quiver. She didn't need to peer into the mirror to know what she'd see. Splotches would creep across her olive complexion like a rash. Her brown eyes would appear red-rimmed. She'd seen the look enough within the past weeks to know what to expect.

"Can I get you anything?" he asked from behind the closed bathroom door.

A moment earlier, the bathroom had sparkled with cleanliness. "Lysol? A sponge?"

"Don't worry about cleaning up. I meant for you. Are you okay?" His voice sounded muffled, but for the first time, it lightened a notch.

She cracked open the bathroom door.

Concern flooded his face. She could almost forget moments ago she nearly lost it on his Nikes.

"Are you ill? Carsick?" he asked.

"No, not ill." Though, the three-hour drive from her Milwaukee apartment probably hadn't helped.

She rested against the doorframe. Fatigue pumped through her blood.

Maybe those faint lines near his mouth that hinted at a lifetime of smiles made her words want to tumble. "You can trust my cousin Pierce," David had said in his letter. The next words escaped her mouth before she could stop them.

"I'm...I'm pregnant." There, she disclosed her miracle to this stranger.

Silence made the air more stifling. Perspiration slithered down her spine and settled into the small of her back. A new wave of nausea jitterbugged in her stomach. Please, no, not again.

"Ah, pregnant." Something flickered across his face, and it wasn't anything like the joy that bubbled inside of her. "Did David know before..." His glance traveled to her trim waistline.

"Yes. He knew." Pierce didn't need to learn about the words sharper than a knife's point that David had flung when he heard the news. Her chin lifted. The back of her skirt stuck to her thighs, and she yanked the material free with a snap. Involuntarily, her shoulders squared. His next words would determine her baby's future relationship with the child's extended family.

"Congratulations on the baby." His voice sounded as flat as the Illinois cornfields she had driven past. "Does my aunt know?"

Kendra shook her head. No, but now he knew about her little miracle. She needed to tell his aunt as soon as possible. "Only you do, for now."

"Let's keep it that way."

Now it was her turn to frown. "Why, I—"

"Do you have family who will help you?"

She touched her fingers to the heart-shaped locket she always wore that used to be her mom's. Outside, a car rumbled and cut through her thoughts. She twirled a loose curl through her fingers, a nervous habit she had given up years ago. She had no other choice but to put this cherished baby first and move forward.

"I'll be a single mom." She said the words without hesitation. "I'll succeed. Look how well I'm doing." With a smile, she flared her skirt and curtsied. By his expression, her attempt to lift the mood with a joke fell flat. Truth would work better. She let her skirt fall free. "I love this baby already more than I ever thought possible. I come from a long line of strong women, and I'll surround this baby with love and wrap this child in a blanket of faith and kindness."

He lifted his eyebrows. "Be independent. Don't bother my aunt about this and the money, not now."

Yes, she was strong and independent. Nothing he could have said about her and her family could've been truer. Didn't he realize she needed that money for her baby's sake, not for a shoe-shopping spree at Macy's?

Kendra peered up at him. "I came here now because the library I work for is closed for two months. Yesterday was my last day as they begin construction. My pay...Anyways..." He didn't need to know her troubles that she'd work out. She could stride toward the front door, could turn around and leave. Pierce wouldn't bother to tell his aunt about her visit. The idea of family, a real family, tugged at her. Kept her rooted in place. "Your aunt said..."

She hoped it didn't sound like she blamed his aunt. Of course, Mrs. McFarland would be thrilled to see her. Wait until his aunt learned about the baby. Her mother-in-law would be amazed. This tiny life thrived inside her, changing and growing each day. After Kendra and Mrs. McFarland befriended one another, maybe over a cup of decaffeinated tea, sliced strawberries, and freshly baked blueberry muffins, she'd ask. Mrs. McFarland had to know where David kept the funds he wanted his wife and baby to have, even if Kendra's late husband had wanted nothing to do with the child. She swallowed hard at that fact.

He cleared his throat. "Although David isn't with us any longer, we'll welcome this baby."

She licked her lips, waiting. The words she wanted and dreamed she'd hear never came: "We'll welcome *you* to our family."

Especially today, hormones burst through her like a Fourth of July firecracker finale. No way would she let a single tear tumble.

From the kitchen, a buzzer rang. With his back turned, she touched the corner of her mouth. Her cheeks ached from all the emotions bubbling inside her. She couldn't remember the last day that happened. Perhaps, the morning she first learned about her pregnancy. She had danced around her apartment, wishing her mom or dad were still alive to call with the news. Her lips being stuck in an all-day smile had made her cheeks throb. Nothing had ever felt so good.

"You'll be okay in the kitchen? Cinnamon rolls baking. Will that make you sick? You could wait in the living room."

The kitchen might include a ceiling fan to move the air. She could hope anyways. "I'm better now. Thanks." His consideration about the baby helped her hands stop trembling.

In contrast with the dark and dreary living room, the kitchen shone bright with sunny yellow walls. The scent of baking rolls caused her to breathe in and capture the scrumptious smell. Her stomach rumbled loud enough for him to hear; well, for anyone in Shallow Stream to hear.

Two steps into the kitchen, she gasped with delight. Her whole apartment could fit into this expansive room. If she lived in this farmhouse, she'd spend every possible moment puttering about here. A sunflower-design tablecloth rested beneath two pewter candleholders. Next to the candles, a plate overflowed with red grapes. Apples glistened in an etched glass bowl like a scene out of a still-life painting.

He closed the oven door. "I put these in the oven right before I headed out for my quick run. I promised my aunt she could rest, and I wouldn't be gone long. They're not quite done."

She fidgeted in the kitchen chair once she sat down. The chair's spindles poked at her sky-blue blouse that topped her floral skirt. After trying on five or six outfits to locate which one proclaimed "responsible mom-to-be," she had made her final clothing choice. Though she'd skipped her boring beige work pumps. Only one answer existed for her footwear choice. Her sandals, bright, shiny, and electric blue, reflected her personality broadcasted on her feet. Fun mom, here we come.

He placed a cold mug of apple cider before her that chilled her hands. "Try this. Made fresh from our orchard's apples." Looking over his shoulder, he lowered his voice. "I bet it cures afternoon sickness. Is that a term?" He shrugged. "I thought it happened only in the morning. Shows what I know."

Morning, noon, and night "sickness," but she wouldn't complain or even label it as an illness. It would all be worth it when she cradled her little one in her arms.

The scent of the baking sweets made her swoon. To her relief, her stomach approved too. "Smells delicious. Yum." Her desire for sweets made a major uptick once she became pregnant. She only needed to see a coconut donut or one dribbled with chocolate. Kendra swore her hand grabbed for that type of treat involuntarily.

"Your aunt bakes?" David's mom couldn't be the barracuda he had made her out to be. Not if she baked for her nephew. What a sweetheart. Kendra couldn't wait to meet a loving mom so dedicated to her family.

Pierce leaned against the spotless granite countertop, and he looked as comfortable as she felt within the Milwaukee library where she worked. Yet, his appraisal of her still lingered and made her squirm. She should've snatched back the letter. Not let him read it so soon. Or better yet, stayed quiet about the whole matter.

"I do the cleaning, cooking, and baking now. For the last two months of the school year, I brought the leftovers to the school where I work. That made me a hero with the rest of the staff. My baking earned me job security," he joked.

She pictured a teacher's lounge filled with sweet scents that would rival any bakery.

"You live here in the house?" She hoped not. He seemed a little old for that.

"I rent an apartment in town near school. Since David's death, I've been staying in the cottage on the property."

He pointed out the window. Standing, she peeked through the white lace kitchen curtains. She spotted the yellow-painted cabin, cute as a dollhouse but more masculine looking with the maroon shutters and window boxes that overflowed with some kind of leafy vines.

"I'll be nearby until my aunt gets stronger. She can't handle any additional stress." He gave her a warning look.

Kendra raised her eyebrows. She knew what she needed, too. She wouldn't back down. Not when her baby's wellbeing mattered, and that took priority over everything.

"Baking and running relax me. I figured something homemade might cheer my aunt up. Keep her from staying in bed most of the day. If only it were that easy."

When her dad had died, her mom had no other choice but to go to work. With a young daughter to support, staying in bed had never been an option.

He grabbed a pair of oven mitts and checked the rolls with a jab of the fork. "Done, golden brown." Then, he yanked the baking sheet from the oven. A cinnamon scent burst through the kitchen. "Sure you can eat one?"

She stopped herself from grabbing a roll right from the hot baking sheet. "Can't resist." That was an understatement. On cue, her stomach rumbled.

He handed her a china dish edged with purple pansies that held a cinnamon roll the size of her palm. His strong hands contrasted with the delicate plate.

"Still hot," she mumbled as the cinnamon tiptoed along her tongue. "Delicious." After she nibbled the first roll, she wanted to gulp down a second one. To keep from grabbing it, she sat on her right hand. Her baby needed fruits and vegetables, not more sweets, no matter how scrumptious the roll tasted. "May I have your recipe, or do you stow it away in some secret vault?"

"It's a McFarland family secret, but you claim we're family now."

"Claim" made her bite her lip and study the linoleum. Still, family, everything she wanted for her precious baby from the moment the doctor confirmed her pregnancy. She imagined Thanksgiving visits with platters of turkey, crescent rolls, and corn casseroles. She'd bring her artichoke dip—always a big hit. Although the frosting could be tricky depending on the weather, she could also tote a homemade Texas sheet cake.

The holidays appeared so real in her thoughts she could almost reach out and grab them. Christmas memories made in front of a fir tree with children's laughter and Christmas carols filling the living room as the family joined together and celebrated their faith. Handcrafted ornaments would clink and jostle as the children rushed by the tree. The evergreen scent would perfume the air. Maybe they'd head toward town and carol through the neighborhood. Then again, if they heard Kendra's singing voice, worse than a crow's caw, that might not be the best idea.

Everything wonderful her own family enjoyed disappeared for her at age ten after her dad died of pancreatic cancer. With no other choice, her mom left her alone on every holiday to work two jobs. Kendra's child would never experience such hardships; she'd make certain of it. Somehow.

Yes, she wanted family. She also hoped for closure about David. Her three-month marriage included every insult her late husband could shout. The words stabbed at her with a strength that equaled any cut from a knife. No, she wasn't "fat," "ugly," "worthless," or "stupid." She wanted to erase those memories and start a life so shiny and new, she could forget his cruel words. Every night of her marriage she'd reminded herself of her inner strength with prayers and Bible verses that affirmed God's love.

"Pierce, are you there?" a woman's voice called.

"We're down here in the kitchen," he said.

"We're?" Mrs. McFarland's voice escalated an octave.

"Join us," Pierce added.

Kendra sat up straighter in the kitchen chair and couldn't stop smiling. In a moment, she'd meet her baby's grandma. With a family, all the broken pieces of her life would fit together.

10

Chapter Two

The base of Pierce's neck pulsated as if a giant hand squeezed. He should've skipped the baking. Gone for his usual run instead. The ache in his legs and the whoosh of air expanding his lungs didn't equal the peace he had in life prior to his cousin's death when everything changed.

Nothing would help his aunt either, except seeing David alive. That wouldn't—couldn't happen. Questions tugged at his heart. He should've been direct. "My aunt is sad. Seeing you here is the last thing she needs. For some reason, I suspect she blames you for her son's death." Why would Aunt Meryl think this? He had no clue. This was the first time he ever admitted that suspicion. His aunt wouldn't give him any details for her misplaced anger against her daughter-in-law. Meeting Kendra wouldn't help his aunt. That much he knew.

Aunt Meryl inviting Kendra to the farmhouse seemed as likely as him coming in first place in the New York City Marathon. The pregnancy shocked him even more. David had always stated he didn't want kids of his own. Not ever. His aunt knew that fact.

That letter she had brought? Well, that ranked as an even bigger surprise. Those words ripped through his bones. He assumed she planned to treasure hunt through the house. No way would that happen. He'd stop her. Even if it meant he'd pull an all-nighter while listening to the tick-tock of the grandfather clock. He pictured his aunt discovering Kendra riffling through drawers. Checking under the beds. He imagined his aunt's shouts pounding through his ears, before ricocheting through the house. Then, Aunt Meryl would fist her hands at her sides right before she'd burst with a fury rivaling any volcano. Her eyes would bug and go wide. His aunt's expression looked like that a lot lately. Like her son, Aunt Meryl's anger erupted without warning

Nope, he couldn't let Kendra begin her prize search. Right before David left Shallow Stream, he had made his cousin a promise. No matter what happened, he'd watch over his aunt. His cousin wouldn't have to worry. Pierce wouldn't break that promise. Although he didn't know it then, that pledge would be the last words he'd ever say to his cousin, who was the younger brother he had never had. He owed it to David and his aunt to keep his word.

"What's she like?" Kendra whispered, interrupting his thoughts.

"She'll be here in a second. See for yourself." Then, as his aunt's temper ignited and burned hot enough to set the farmhouse aflame, Kendra would leave. That would be for the best.

If he could, he'd whip out his checkbook, and then grab a pen. Write Kendra a check for whatever funds she needed for the baby. Unfortunately, that couldn't happen. When Pierce read the letter Kendra showed him, Lacey Randall popped into his mind. After he slid an engagement ring on Lacey's slender finger seven months ago, she had calculated a high school counselor's salary. For her, the numbers didn't add up. Her final text message still burned his gut: "I need someone who can support me at the high level I'm used to." Which he assumed would be the Gross Domestic Product for Luxembourg.

~~~~~

Standing in the hallway at the edge of the staircase, Kendra wanted to peek at David's mom before the woman saw her. In her emails, Mrs. McFarland had ignored Kendra's cheery, "Enjoy your day!" She expected Mrs. McFarland to be dressed in all black. The woman's spine would look straight and strong. Perhaps her hair would be pulled back into a tightly wound chignon that would give her an air of sophistication. As Mrs. McFarland shuffled down the stairs, Kendra spied her.

Other than the worn slippers, faded black leggings with a tattered hem, and baggy Bears' T-shirt, Mrs. McFarland seemed okay. Could she be faulted for dressing in comfy clothes on a stormy Sunday afternoon? Kendra did it often.

Her body tingled with excitement. After all this time, she'd meet her mother-in-law. Family would fill the emptiness that gurgled inside her so loudly she assumed everyone heard. "Hi, I'm Kendra." She leaned forward, smiled, and held out her hand.

After taking the last stair to the first floor, Mrs. McFarland stared up at her. A scent like a waterlogged library book caused Kendra's pregnant stomach to quiver. Close up, the woman's dark hair hung limply. White streaks in her hair framed her face and aged her by ten years. Dark circles shadowed the woman's eyes.

"Do I know you?" Mrs. McFarland asked. The flat tone made Kendra tremble.

"You don't, but I'm David's wife." Now that Mrs. McFarland realized who she was, it would be the right time to hug her. Kendra held out her arms. The woman didn't move forward. Mrs. McFarland looked at her as if she were some scarecrow. Kendra dropped her empty arms to her side. She expected Mrs. McFarland to smile or nod or something. Anything but continue to stare at her blankly.

"We emailed. You invited me here today. Then, you told me the

12

whole family would visit too." Her voice became higher and squeakier with each sentence. Ever since her first email to Mrs. McFarland, Kendra couldn't think of much else other than proclaiming: "You're going to be a grandma. Congrats!" She bit her lip to keep from shouting the words.

"I'm your daughter-in-law."

"My beloved David is dead. My son would've wanted a proper, church wedding, and, most certainly, he would've invited the family," Mrs. McFarland said.

Kendra stepped backward and sat down. Was she serious? He most certainly did marry. She owned the gold wedding band and Marquise-cut diamond engagement ring she and David had picked out together at Lanier Gems as proof. She rubbed her finger across the engagement ring she still wore. What was wrong with this woman? Of course, she mourned, but to doubt Kendra's word teetered on her being unhinged. She told Mrs. McFarland in one of the emails she and David had married. Mrs. McFarland — no way could she call her "mom" — even typed back, "Congratulations." An exclamation mark would've made it better, but, still, Kendra had beamed and stared at her computer for half an hour after she had received that email.

She fidgeted in the kitchen chair. A terrible thought tugged at her. Mrs. McFarland might demand proof of the marriage. Who'd ask for documentation as though she was applying for a passport rather than visiting her late husband's family? The heat climbed down her neck. It settled like a too-tight necklace, pinching her throat.

Taking a deep breath, she hoped to steady her voice. "We married at the courthouse before he left for overseas. For his new job," Kendra added. She didn't want anyone guessing David left the country because of her.

At the mention of the courthouse, the corner of Mrs. McFarland's mouth twitched. Kendra could relate. No, there had not been a ceremony in her community church with Pastor James smiling at her. No frothy-white wedding of her dreams, complete with a rose bridal bouquet and bridesmaids in matching peach-colored dresses. Instead, a city clerk yawned throughout the ceremony and checked the wall clock twice. Despite the warm courtroom, goose bumps had dotted her forearms. She had bought David a boutonniere that took her an hour to select, but her hands remained empty throughout the ceremony. While David took her tears as her being overcome with joy, the truth made her heart ache.

"You married at the courthouse?" Mrs. McFarland shook her head. "That would never happen. My Davey wouldn't have let that occur."

Kendra bit her bottom lip. "I wanted a church wedding more than anything, but David had to leave and --"

"He's dead," the woman interrupted. Her eyes blanked, and her face dulled. "I'll never see my son again. What matters beyond that fact?"

"I know. I'm so sorry." She stood next to her mother-in-law and tried to hold her hand. Her own fingers shook. She had to do something to comfort this poor, grieving woman. Kendra couldn't imagine any mother's pain about her child dying before her, sadness no mom should endure. She placed her arm around the woman's shoulders.

Mrs. McFarland yanked out of her reach as if Kendra's touch scorched her. Then, she leaned against the chair. Any moment, the woman would topple. The inside of Kendra's throat turned to dust. She couldn't meet Pierce's eyes. Her mother-in-law would rather risk injury than accept her comfort.

Pierce cleared his throat. "Please sit down, Aunt Meryl. You knew that David married Kendra, and you told me this yourself." His deep voice helped quiet her too-fast breathing. "You seem to be forgetting facts."

Mrs. McFarland raised her eyebrows but said nothing. Kendra recalled a rainy morning in second grade when she stood at the white board in front of her classmates, while the math problem in front of her morphed into a foreign language she didn't understand. This reminded her of that moment.

Then, she remembered something that would help. She carried with her the perfect gifts to improve this meeting. They'd smooth over the hurt feelings. Her heart skipped a beat. Everything would work out. She even managed a smile, a real smile that made her cheeks throb.

"This is for you." She reached for her blue tote bag with a shaking hand. "I love to knit. I didn't know your favorite color." David never mentioned anything specific about his mom. "So I made you a neutral-hued scarf, mittens, and hat. I hope the set will go well with your winter coat." Every Midwest resident could use some help staying warm in the chilly weather. Mrs. McFarland would love these handcrafted presents she now held out to her.

Mrs. McFarland shook her head and pushed against the table. The presents tumbled. Kendra gasped. She plucked the hat from the ground and recalled the hours she knitted until her thumbs throbbed. The yellow bow she had fashioned with care unraveled into a stringy ribbon that fell flat against the tile floor. Pierce grabbed the scarf and mittens that had dangled on the chair's edge.

"Sorry," he said, so low only she could hear. "I'm sure these took Kendra a long time to make for you, Aunt Meryl."

That was for sure. Without looking up, she stuffed each of the items back into the gift bag. Maybe her best friend would enjoy the presents, but it wouldn't be the same as David's mom happily accepting her tokens of love.

"Kendra traveled all the way from Milwaukee, Wisconsin, so you could meet," he added, as he put a plate with a cinnamon roll down on the table in front of his aunt.

"I know where Milwaukee is. I don't need a geography lesson. I never invited her to visit this weekend," Mrs. McFarland said, with a wave of her hand.

Heat burned her cheeks. The woman should care about her only son's widow. Even more, Kendra expected her grandchild. If Mrs. McFarland knew, would it change her reaction? For now, she'd abide by Pierce's request and stay quiet about the pregnancy.

"You did invite me." She reached for her phone and searched for the emails she had shown Pierce. The ones that would confirm the invitation, complete with date and time.

In a single step, his long-legged stride brought him to his aunt's side. "I've seen the emails from Kendra's phone, Aunt Meryl. Kendra is correct that you invited her today, and you promised she could meet the entire family."

The woman shrugged. "I...must have forgotten. I don't remember well anymore. One day melts into the next." She looked away.

He turned to Kendra. "It doesn't matter. You're here." It did matter, to her at least. His aunt believed Kendra pushed herself into the farmhouse and into their lives. She'd never be so rude. Kendra forced herself to hold back the words rather than heat up the confrontation. She slunk back into the chair, the spindles sharp against her back.

"Did you ride David's motorcycle here?" the woman asked.

Since when did David own a motorcycle? "No, of course not, I'm..."

At Pierce's sharp look, she stopped herself from finishing the sentence.

What motorcycle? "I didn't know David even rode a motorcycle. Maybe it's stashed in storage? I'll check." Although she welcomed adventures, hopping on a Harley didn't appear anywhere on her bucket list. She imagined bugs smashing against her goggles. She pictured traffic zooming around her without the safety of car doors.

Mrs. McFarland's eyebrows shot up so high Kendra expected them to disappear into her hairline.

"He wouldn't put his motorcycle in storage," she said, each word an attack.

Kendra frowned. She didn't want to further upset Mrs. McFarland.

Though this time, she couldn't remain silent. "I didn't know his bike existed."

"If you knew my son, you'd know about his beloved motorcycle. Davey spent half his time buffing it to a sheen," Mrs. McFarland added.

Tightness squeezed her shoulders. Davey? She shuddered. Her late husband never allowed that nickname.

"Maybe he sold it right before we met?" She was about to ask about the last time Mrs. McFarland had seen her son. From what she could piece together, about a dozen years had passed since he left the farmhouse behind and didn't glance back.

"Never would he sell his prized bike," Mrs. McFarland said.

Could a motorcycle mean so much? It was only a thing, not a person. People sold vehicles all the time without a second thought.

"I'm done eating." She handed the full plate back to her nephew. Her napkin perched in the middle of the plate like an exclamation point.

"Your doctor said," he began.

"I'm going back to bed. I faced another sleepless night while I remembered my son."

Kendra stood. Compassion bubbled through her, despite her mother-in-law's rudeness. She needed to do something to acknowledge Mrs. McFarland's feelings. The poor woman. Grief seeped into every moment of her life, night and day.

"The doctor also said I need rest. Let's not argue in front of her," Mrs. McFarland said.

Her? Kendra blinked hard. She pictured the future times she'd need to be strong, raising her baby alone. Glancing at Pierce, she checked his reaction. No surprise as much as she could see. Did his aunt always act so impolitely?

"Stay and chat with us." Pierce placed a hand on his aunt's shoulder as if he held her in place.

"Too tired. Maybe more sleep would help me remember better."

Kendra swallowed hard as she waited for an apology that never came.

Mrs. McFarland gazed past the kitchen curtains as though she wished she could be anywhere else other than across the table from her daughter-in-law. "No one is left for me." Without a second glance or another word, she stood and passed by Kendra.

"You have Pierce." Sure, it wasn't any of her business, but she didn't like the hurt look that flickered across his face. She guessed by the spotless kitchen Pierce also scrubbed the tile to a shine and made the granite countertops glisten. The guy worked a full-time job. He probably didn't have to go into the high school much during the summer, but her teacher acquaintances still attended curriculum school meetings throughout their off months. Mrs. McFarland glared back at her a final time. Kendra refused to back down. "You're lucky he helps you."

"I am certainly not lucky." The harshness of the woman's words rivaled a lion's roar.

Uh-oh. Kendra leaned against the edge of the kitchen table to steady herself for the next argument. "With the bad weather, may I stay here tonight?" The dollar bills in her wallet wouldn't pay for even half of a hotel room. In her last email, Mrs. McFarland had offered...well, it didn't matter.

The woman's shoulders slumped. "I wouldn't send you out in this storm."

Frustration bubbled inside her. Keep quiet. The words burst out anyway. "Is that the only reason you're letting me stay?" Either Mrs. McFarland would lie, or the answer would be like a slap. Both options would sting.

"Yes, that's the reason," Mrs. McFarland said.

She should have kept her mouth closed.

"Remember this is your son's *wife* you're speaking to. You owe Kendra an apology." Arms crossed, Pierce blocked his aunt's shuffle to the staircase.

"Sorry." Mrs. McFarland's eyes flashed the flat color of pebbles.

No, Mrs. McFarland wasn't one bit sorry. Kendra hoped she could soften the grief's sharp edges with phone calls, cheery cards, and visits. No way would she find the loving family she dreamed of within this farmhouse.

Chapter Three

The next morning, Kendra pulled herself out of bed with a groan. Always up in time to appreciate the sunrise's majesty, the clock on the nightstand had to be wrong. It couldn't be nine o'clock. The day was a quarter over already. Her head thundered like the storm clouds that brewed last night.

A glance at the framed pictures crowding the dresser made her remember her location. The photo of David, smiling and carefree, stared back at her. She considered placing it face down, but she couldn't bring herself to be that rude. What explanation would she give if Pierce, or even worse, Mrs. McFarland spotted the overturned photo? She didn't need to add to the family's sadness.

"You really loved motorcycles that much?" What other important things had he failed to tell her? "In the end, you certainly didn't love me, and you definitely didn't love this baby." The cruel words he used toward her after they married jabbed at her like an endless recording she couldn't turn off. Thank goodness the baby would never hear those insults. She rubbed her hand protectively across her stomach. "My baby."

The sleepless night made her crave crackers and ginger ale. It would be one of those mornings. She forced herself to shower and dress, though her stomach lurched each time she took a step.

"Hey, good morning," Pierce said, when she arrived in the kitchen. A smile replaced his frown. "Sorry about last evening. I don't know what got into my aunt. She has a bad temper sometimes, but she's not normally unkind. It was like I didn't know her."

Kendra could relate.

"Ever since David…" he began.

"I know." The less said about her late husband, the better. She started to wave her hand, then she remembered: Mrs. McFarland had used that same motion to dismiss her.

Without the tapping of the rain from yesterday, the house came alive. When Pierce walked, the white tile squeaked under each sock-wearing step. The breeze rattled the window screens. For most of his life, her late husband spent meals gathered with his parents at this very table. That fact should've tugged at her heart and make her say, "awww."

Instead, she turned to Pierce. "The beef stew you cooked tasted delicious at dinner last night." This time, she refrained from asking for the recipe in case he labeled it another family secret.

"Glad you enjoyed the meal. That leads us into breakfast. What would you like to eat? An omelet? Pancakes? Maple sausage?"

Her stomach flipped. Eggs ranked as the last thing her belly craved. The look on his face told her he tried to make up for his aunt's behavior. Part of her wanted to deny him this chance after the way his aunt had treated her. Maybe the woman in her grief did forget the date. She needed to give Mrs. McFarland the benefit of the doubt.

For now, her pregnancy stomach betrayed her and took breakfast food off the list of options. "Is a good night's sleep on the menu?" she asked, joking. "Does your gourmet breakfast menu include saltine crackers?"

He got up from the kitchen table and returned the strawberry jam to the refrigerator's shelves. "Let me know if I can make you something else later."

"Okay, you've been more than kind. This morning anyway," she added, to make certain he hadn't forgotten the lawyer-like inquisition from the day before. Why she didn't experience nightmares, she'd never know. This morning that witness stand that trapped her yesterday dissolved. Today, a smile replaced his rapid-fire questions.

"Let me return the favor and do the dishes when we're done eating. Then you can show me your delightful town. It looked pretty as a postcard. I strolled past a coffee shop, a fresh fruit market, and a real estate office on the corner of Main and Ridge avenues called Martin Realty."

"Yes, that's Joel Martin's business. My sister worked for him for a few years."

"Oh. Does this town have an antique store? I didn't spot one." Perusing antique stores—what could be a better way to spend an afternoon?

He beamed as if she asked him the very question he'd waited and wanted to hear. "We have *two* antique stores. What's Old is New Again and Andy's Antique Treasures. The owners compete against each other. If I visit one store, I have to stop in the other. They keep track. You like antiques?"

She smiled at his hopeful expression that seemed as if he'd planned to give someone tours of both stores and had been hoping for her to spring the question. "I love to imagine the stories behind old things." She had pictured who owned that blue bowl with the scalloped edge in the front window of the antique store near her Milwaukee apartment. Where the objects existed in their homes, on the kitchen table for everyone to use or stashed away in a curio. What trinkets meant to the owners. "Such fun."

"Wear your watch. I'll take you to each establishment for an equal amount of time. Then the shop owners can't accuse me of favoritism."

She nibbled the crackers he set before her. To her relief, her stomach stopped roiling. "I'll do the dishes before we leave for our Shallow Stream adventure."

"You're the guest. Forget about dishwashing. Guests don't scrub dishes."

She raised her eyebrows. "I'm also family," she reminded him and hoped he'd agree. She needed to say that word aloud. Family. With everything that had happened with his aunt, this didn't feel like the family she had prayed she'd join.

That made her remember. "Oh no, I skipped my morning prayer." No wonder her day started off wrong. She placed her hand to her neck and hoped her pregnancy-induced forgetfulness would soon end. "Would you pray with me? It would set the day back on the right track."

He cleared this throat. "Since David's death, I don't do things like that anymore. It doesn't work. Prayer."

"Now's a great time to start, praying I mean." Tucking the kitchen chair under the table, she stood next to him.

~~~~~

Could Pierce deny her a prayer to start her day? It seemed like a simple request, but it shoved against his ribs like a pulled muscle from running too far, too fast.

"I'd rather not." Yes, prayer used to calm him. But he didn't need to relax. Everything clicked along fine for him. Why bother?

She reached for his hand. The warmth of her fingers coaxed his clenched fist to open. Her eyes shone with anticipation of her body relaxing.

"I'll pray then. You can listen...or not."

He tried the "or not" option. He didn't need this. He had his high school students to worry about and a conference he'd attend in late September. When she squeezed his hand, the energy traveled up his arm like a gentle hug. Warmth and love radiated off her like the early morning heat.

"Dear God, thank You for this glorious day with the sun shining after the storms. You always give us hope in the most challenging of times. We thank You for all of our many blessings. We remain grateful for another day to show others Your love through our own kindness. Amen."

Soon, Kendra would be a single mom, which had to include

challenges. His life watching over his aunt, even when she snarled, wasn't that difficult. It wouldn't be forever. Eventually, Aunt Meryl would feel better. Maybe she'd even forgive Kendra for whatever she imagined her daughter-in-law did wrong. His aunt wouldn't need him so much. Despite what his former fiancée claimed, he had a career that mattered more than a fat bank account. The students at Washington High counted on him to listen to their worries of not getting straight A's. Most of his fellow teachers he'd call "friend." Many, even in Shallow Stream, had it worse. He had much to be grateful for too. Despite feeling about as comfortable as attending a black-tie event wearing his workout gear, he said the words and breathed along with her.

After the prayer, the tension in his neck loosened like that always-there knot was being untied. "Amen." To his surprise, praying had been easier than expected.

Letting go of her hand, he turned toward the stove. "Hey, how are those crackers going down?" He grabbed the skillet. "What about scrambled eggs and dry wheat toast? It's blah, but at least real food."

"Thanks, I can handle the dry toast, but please let's skip the eggs. Where's your aunt? Won't she eat breakfast?"

Kendra glanced toward the stairway as though Aunt Meryl would swoop in any moment, armed with an arsenal of new insults. Facing his aunt across the breakfast table might make Kendra lose her appetite altogether.

"She sleeps. A lot now." Way too much, and he wished he knew how to keep her up throughout the day. The beef stew he tried last night to coax her to the dinner table didn't work. Today, he'd think up something new, something besides a hearty meal.

Right now, he had a guest to entertain, and he owed it to his late cousin to be a gracious host. In addition, he couldn't chance Kendra starting her treasure hunt for the money alone. He paused as he cracked an egg, one-handed, to cook for himself.

Kendra gave him a thumbs-up. "Cool trick. Sure you don't teach home ec?"

"My high school doesn't offer the class anymore." Lots had changed in the last two years. His perfect wife-to-be disappeared. With her "goodbye and good luck, no hard feelings" text, Lacey squashed his view of love. But he didn't want to think about Lacey, especially when he glanced over at Kendra. Her skin looked dewy. Pregnancy made her face glimmer. Light from the kitchen window gleamed across her light brown curls. Even more, Kendra's inner strength shone when she managed to stay calm under Aunt Meryl's fury. That ranked as quite a feat. He owed Kendra some kindness in return.

"What do you say about an afternoon in Shallow Stream? Think about it. I can tell you some family secrets along the way." He waggled his eyebrows in a way to intrigue her or at least make her giggle.

She coughed in response. Either the crusty wheat toast or the words "family secrets" made her choke. He guessed "family."

While waiting for Kendra's response, he wrapped up the leftover blueberry pancakes he made earlier and stashed them in the refrigerator with a note for his aunt. Not that she'd eat them. Did his aunt forget Kendra's arranged visit? He'd never know. Although his aunt seemed unusually sharp-tongued the previous evening, she always managed accurate insights about people. No doubt Aunt Meryl despised Kendra with every ounce of her being.

Still, Kendra didn't know about the motorcycle. That fact made him toss and turn throughout the night. This morning he found the two pillows that should've been under his head flung across the room. Sleeping in David's old room with his cousin's letterman jacket hung in the closet and his wrestling trophies perched on top of the dresser like a shrine didn't help.

What had happened to his cousin's prized bike? That ranked as the million-dollar question. Each weekend morning, David had peeled off to ride his motorcycle, revving through the town's back roads. Kendra knew nothing about her husband's most beloved possession and hobby.

"Feel better after eating?" he asked. Without his aunt in sight, that was a given.

"I'm much better thanks to you. I'm ready to go and see your and uh…David's town."

His school counselor's job prepared him well for keeping a face as blank as an unused computer screen. Not once had Kendra uttered her late husband's name without cringing. Not a single time. She spat out David's name like it tasted terrible. Everyone handled death differently. Maybe she resented his cousin for dying and leaving her a young, pregnant widow. Pierce couldn't imagine the tsunami of emotions that swept through her. He certainly had no right to judge.

"Maybe you want to take a run first," she said.

Any time he reached for his running shoes, Lacey had complained he wasn't spending enough time with her. "I'm good. I'll run later. The town won't go anywhere, but our famous festival ends soon. Want to go to the Summer Festival that put Shallow Stream on the map?"

She laughed, and her eyes lit up in a way that captured him. His heart jolted, but he ignored his reaction. His aunt needed him 24/7. That was where his focus would remain.

"I had a hard time finding this place. I'm not sure Shallow Stream appears on any map. Going to the festival sounds like fun."

He nodded. "Let me scribble a note to my aunt so she doesn't worry." Or have something else to complain about that involved Kendra.

Everyone loved their town's festival with face painting, popcorn, corn-on-the-cob, carnival rides, games, and crafts. Pierce would get to know Kendra better. Nothing could go wrong at the Fest.

Chapter Four

Stepping up into Pierce's fire-red Jeep, Kendra wracked her brain. Think, think. Her late husband had uttered less than a sentence about his family. And he hadn't muttered a single word about his hometown. If he did, Kendra couldn't recall. She should've asked him more questions about his time growing up. That was what dating couples did. But their relationship progressed like a whirlwind. She recalled behavior like that Saturday, the first week after they married. After he'd emptied out their savings account and bought gardening tools and a lawn mower, when their apartment payment included landscaping. With cheeks that burned, she had returned the items. When she returned empty-handed, he'd shouted at her and called her "controlling." Her heart sank at that memory. His home-baked oatmeal cookies, chats in front of the flickering fireplace, and evening strolls along Lake Michigan only occurred before they married. Once they said, "I do," their relationship plunged into the chill of a nightmare from which she never awoke.

How unusual this must look to the McFarland family. She had to admit she'd married a stranger. She didn't know his lifelong dream, favorite color, best subject in school, or his most embarrassing childhood memory. In fact, she could rattle off more facts about Mrs. Syed, her landlord who lived in the first-floor apartment in Milwaukee, than she could about her late husband.

Even more, she had no idea where he would've hidden that money. Could it be in his old bedroom that Pierce slept in last night? How could she gain access to the room? Pierce watched her every move. Even if she did manage to sneak into the room, where would she start to look? What if Mrs. McFarland caught her? She shivered. Besides, she didn't have the mind of a thief. Yet, the money belonged to her. The funds she'd need when her baby arrived and she had to pay for diapers and daycare. Taking a deep breath, she vowed to find the cash for her child, even if she had to scour the house on tiptoe at midnight.

"That's our high school. Washington." He slowed the Jeep and pointed to the redbrick building. It stood a third of the size of her former high school in Milwaukee. "Go Ramblers," a white and purple sign proclaimed over the school's entryway.

"David went there too?" She had no idea.

"When he showed up." He shrugged, whether from embarrassment or defeat, she didn't know.

"Washington High School is also where I work," he added.

Pride filled his voice.

"You never left your hometown?" It must be one special place for him to stay here all those years. David had set out the day after high school graduation and never looked backward.

"For a short while, I did. I wanted to see if I missed anything by living in a small town. Then I returned. I saw what I gave up by living in Chicago. I made more money in the city, but I missed the sense of community our small town offers. I like to know my neighbors' names."

She nodded. Other than her landlord, she knew few people in her Milwaukee neighborhood. Kendra could count how many library patrons' names she knew, despite her efforts. How wonderful to meet and care for people who lived near her. "How'd your cousin act in high school?" Maybe if she learned about him, she could bury her anger about how she'd been treated during their short marriage. It raged inside her with the heat of a forest fire. If for no other reason, if she let the fury go, the baby couldn't sense her pain.

"He played sports. Wrestling, track, and football. Less academics, much less. My cousin defined underachiever. But he had so much potential." Pierce cleared his throat at the last sentence. Then he looked straight ahead as he answered this question, as though his response brought back bad memories.

Their love of sports ranked as one thing David and Kendra had in common, maybe all they shared.

"What about you?"

Unlike his aunt, at least this morning he acted as though he wanted to get to know her. She might have one McFarland relative who didn't despise her. Better than none.

"Not much," he said. "I spent most of my time checking up on..."

"Stop!"

Pierce slammed on the brakes. "What? What's wrong?" His gaze went right to her stomach.

She spotted the red and white sign with the giant pizza painted on the side. "Dimorio's. He said he ate at Dimorio's pizza parlor after football games, always pepperoni pizza." She wiggled with excitement in her seat. "Maybe we could eat there for lunch? My treat, oh, except I discovered this morning I accidentally left my credit card and cash at home. Pregnancy has made me so forgetful. I feel like I've lost my mind sometimes. I can pay you back and..." Heat warmed her cheeks, and she put her face in her hands.

He chuckled. "No worries. I'll pay. You're the guest. Remember?"

How could she forget? Not the guest, *family,* she almost corrected him. He had disregarded that fact a few times. Unlike her, he couldn't blame pregnancy for his slip.

She squeezed her hands to keep from doing a fist bump. Yes! She knew something about her late husband. A weight lifted from her chest as though she had won the *Jeopardy* challenge.

~~~~~

He grinned, not about her treating, then realizing she didn't have any cash. He wanted to pull over. Grab his phone. Call his aunt. "See, she said the truth. You doubted her. Told you." Although his aunt hadn't accused Kendra of anything directly, Aunt Meryl had somehow developed an instant dislike to Kendra. This time, her spot-on radar fell off course. Relief relaxed the tension his shoulders carried.

Sure, Kendra could've looked up Dimorio's on the Internet. Yet, how would she know that after every football game, win or lose, they all piled into the pizza parlor a block from the high school? That wouldn't be included on the restaurant's site. Only residents of Shallow Stream knew that fact.

His hands relaxed, and he hadn't even realized that he had clutched the steering wheel. That knot in the back of his neck unfurled.

"That'd be fun to eat at Dimorio's. The students still visit the restaurant after each football game," he said. "Not now. School's out for the summer."

"Is that okay, that you'd run into students today?"

"Summer is different around here. Students pop up everywhere." Then he realized what she meant and cringed. He never had a woman at his side who wasn't his sister. Since the break-up with Lacey, which the entire town knew about, he'd taken a hiatus from dating. Everyone in town would assume...even Kendra guessed what they'd assume. At least once per month one of his students tried to fix him up. Get him to date. The list of older cousins and never-married aunts remained endless for such a small town.

At the stoplight, he glanced at Kendra. Sunlight brightened her face. A single curl broke free from her braid and fell in a spiral against her cheek. Forcing himself to take a deep breath, he looked away. He couldn't think that way about any woman. Hadn't he talked to his students who experienced trauma about taking the time to heal? Heeding his own advice ranked as a good move.

"Will everyone talk about you?" she asked.

He hoped not, but sometimes gossip ranked as a spectator sport in his otherwise perfect town. "They can find more interesting things to discuss. You were David's wife. Once they know that, they'll want to talk to *you*." Even though she seemed to know next to nothing about her late husband. "My cousin left our town twelve years ago, but most people in Shallow Stream remember David." Those same people gossiped about the lack of a funeral or memorial service. His aunt topped that list. It accounted for some of her disrespectful behavior toward Kendra.

"Well, we're here. Mind walking?" Putting the Jeep in park, he jogged to her side of the vehicle, opened the door, and held out his hand.

She accepted his help and closed the Jeep's door. "It's a charming town, like out of a movie set. And I'm always up for a walk."

"Great." He guided her over the curb. "Want to start with a snack? You didn't eat much for breakfast. They have an outside food court right off Park Avenue."

"You read my mind. I'm always hungry now. Starving."

"Cravings?"

"Yes, but nothing too strange, popcorn and caramel corn, or caramel corn sprinkled with cheese and seasoned with a handful of jalapeno peppers. You know, those really hot ones."

As they strolled shoulder-to-shoulder, he chuckled. "Nothing too strange." His stomach lurched at the image of caramel corn topped with the sting of red-hot peppers. No wonder she became nauseated.

"Turn here at the corner of Wilson Avenue. You look wobbly." He hooked his arm in hers. She needed his help, that's all. This close, her fragrance made him think sunshine and daisies. He took another deep breath.

"I'm ravenous. I feel like I'm eating for three." She slowed her steps. "You don't think I'm having twins, do you? My doctor doesn't believe in lots of ultrasounds unless something feels wrong."

He clamped his lips closed to keep from offering to pay for an ultrasound, as much as he wanted to do so. Besides, she'd first need to be in contact with her Milwaukee doctor. "I hope you're not pregnant with twins." Even worse. Size-twelve foot inserted in mouth. Wasn't he the guy administrators raved about who could always say the right words to calm distressed students? They called him "eloquent and compassionate." He cleared his throat. Tried to dig himself out of the mess he created. "It would be a bigger challenge. Twins would be twice everything, twice as expensive." By her frown, he realized he should've stayed silent. With every word he said, her chin jutted higher. Her anger sizzled so hot it heated the air.

"I don't have much money with me today. Though I've been good at saving throughout the years."

He looked away, not able to view the holes he unwittingly had punched in her self-esteem. "Don't tell me. It's none of my business."

She didn't need David's money, but with a new baby, it would make her life much easier. That's what she really said. His shoulders relaxed. She could leave today, no problem. No guilt. He'd send her a stand-alone Christmas card with a meaningful sentiment that he carefully selected. Not a Christmas card from a box that he'd send to each of his school's office staff. In addition, he'd make sure he mailed a thoughtful gift as soon as she gave birth. Plus, send flowers with a teddy bear during her hospital stay. That'd be enough, right?

"I didn't mean to pry," he said.

"I'm not destitute." She stopped strolling and placed her arms across her chest. "I want the money David put aside for me, that's all. Nothing more. Money he wanted me, I mean us, to have. Ask anyone who knows me. I'm not materialistic. Okay, I admit I do have an impressive footwear collection, but I use coupons and always buy shoes on sale."

He tried not to laugh, but with her arm no longer linked in his, the situation's humor faded. The space between them plumped with emptiness. Missing her closeness, he jammed his hands deep into his khakis' pockets. With each step, the silence spread, and a barrier pulled them apart.

The sun shimmered through the clouds. Bicycles squealed by on the sidewalk. The breeze smelled of the lilac bushes that many businesses along Main favored. He wouldn't mess this up. Again.

"Hey, look, I didn't mean to invade your space. Your money is your business, not anyone else's. Let's enjoy ourselves." From dating Lacey, he knew too well how money could muddy a relationship, much less a friendship. That was the last thing Kendra needed.

"I smell popcorn," she said. Her voice sounded lighter. "Nothing can be bad if popcorn pops. Isn't that a great sound?"

Now, he laughed. "I never thought of popcorn popping on the list of good sounding things like a waterfall or a raging river." He listened. "You're right. Popcorn popping ranks as a fun and soothing sound with a rhythm and music. Bet someone will realize it and record a song. Maybe you."

"Maybe," she said with a chuckle.

After getting her cheese, regular, and caramel corn with some jalapeno peppers on the side, the color in her cheeks returned.

"How about something to drink?"

She looked up at him. "Sorry I snapped about the money earlier. You've been kind to me...today."

"Ouch. Not so kind yesterday?" She had to understand how strange it had seemed that she arrived at the farmhouse out of the shadows. Plus, she knew about as much about his cousin as he knew about his third-grade teacher whose name he couldn't remember.

"Well, you asked me a lot of questions. Admit it."

True. And if he tried to get her to leave today, that didn't define kindness. The tips of his ears burned.

"You didn't deserve that snippy response about money. I know I'll get questions: 'How will you support a baby on a library circulation supervisor's salary?' That's people, right? They don't mean anything by it. After my belly pops, everyone will ask me all sorts of personal questions." She stared at him through narrowed eyes, as though she dared him to ask one. "I'll manage. My mom did. I can do it too."

He motioned toward a table added for the festival, but she shook her head and kept moving forward.

"Will your mom help with the baby?" She'd seemed so eager to assist his aunt, even when Aunt Meryl acted unkind. Kendra had to have learned compassion somewhere. Church? He hoped her life included someone who would be available after the baby's birth, especially at the beginning.

She touched the silver locket she always wore. "My mom would have helped me. In fact, she'd be here to support me all the way, picking out a crib, shopping for baby clothes, and researching the best car seats." Her eyes glistened. "Throughout my life, she acted as my biggest cheerleader, and we could talk about anything. Well, most things."

Acted. Past tense. He swallowed hard and predicted what would come next.

"My mom died in a car crash almost a year ago now." Her voice shook. "This locket was hers, and it's all I have left of her."

"I'm sorry." She could use someone to help. Kendra must have a best friend, or at least a work colleague, who could step up. She probably had tons of friends.

In the middle of the sidewalk right in front of the green and white-stripped awning of Carlton's Shoes, she paused mid-step. "You don't think I can do this alone. A lot of women do. They manage fine, including my own mom."

He wouldn't question her about who else she had in her life. "Not doubting you one bit." He put up both hands in surrender. "You already love your baby. That's what's most important. If you can think of some way I can help, let me know. My sister called me the baby whisperer when she couldn't calm down her daughters."

"I'll keep that in mind with you living more than three hours away," she said, raising one eyebrow. "Anything is possible if you surround yourself with faith and believe with God's guidance you can succeed."

He cleared his throat. "The faith approach doesn't work for me anymore. I used to think that way too. But I have something in common with my aunt." He paused. Looked into her eyes that reminded him of an open door beckoning him forward. "I'm in a bad place since David's death." There. For the first time, he said the truth instead of lying that he was "fine." He must've used that word a million times. His family expected him to be strong. Take care of everyone else. That was what he did best. Had he known about Kendra's invitation, he would've taken care of the invites without a second thought. That was what Aunt Meryl and everyone else expected. He couldn't believe he admitted this weakness about his sadness to her, especially with what she must be experiencing. Yet, her softened eyes gave him full attention whenever he spoke. Whenever they chatted, he couldn't remember when it had been so easy to talk to anyone.

For a moment, she stayed silent. "I get it. I hope that you've allowed yourself to grieve too. Being everyone's caretaker can be a tough role."

She squeezed his hand. When Kendra looked into his eyes, the stress melted like the dropped ice cream cone he stepped over. She had nailed that one. How could she know him so well when they had only just met? Pierce and his cousin didn't share any personality qualities that allowed her an educated guess about his thoughts, so that couldn't be the reason.

After passing Lynne's Ice Cream Parlor, the Village Baker, and one of the antique shops he mentioned, she pointed to the Shallow Stream Public Library. Located up ahead on the left side of Towne Road, the white brick building with pillars at the entryway stood in the village's center. A garden with tulips bloomed on each side of the library's double doors each spring. Fall, he'd find yellow and maroon mums to replace the tulips. At least once per week, Pierce sat at one of the two benches next to the gardens to read. Had his cousin ever stepped foot inside their community's library? Not on his watch.

"That's how we met." Her words filled the silence that wove in and out between them whenever the memory of his late cousin snuck into their conversation. "He came into the library where I worked in Milwaukee to get a library card. He'd moved to the city and had started to work for Hill's Sporting Goods."

Sporting good sales seemed like a good business for David. Pierce's thoughts plumped to the idea of David finding his niche and succeeding. But his cousin wanted a library card? He held back the cough. His cousin

31

wanted a library card as much as Kendra wanted to forfeit that hidden treasure stashed somewhere within the farmhouse. Other than the back of cereal boxes at breakfast, David didn't read.

He edged them toward one of the library benches. He had to capture each word of this story. The garden's scent filled the air. From the adjoining park, children squealed and giggled.

"What happened when David came into your library?"

"We were about to close for the evening. The light from dusk glinted across the doorway. I remember that so clearly. Then David walked in, and he must have really wanted to check out a book. That impressed me. I thought wow this guy must really be a dedicated reader."

Ah, no.

She stared at the library. "I couldn't send him away."

He pictured his cousin sauntering — the guy never walked — by the library. Most likely, after David spotted Kendra from the sidewalk, he'd decided a library card and her would both be in his future.

"We chatted for an hour at the circulation desk. I should've locked and closed the doors way before then. We...well, clicked," she said.

Her eyes gleamed with the memory.

He winced. They had a fun courtship, but he guessed their marriage hadn't been a happy one. "Did you get in trouble for staying past closing?"

"The library director said she could spot love at first sight. What a romantic, huh?" She smiled at the memory and brought both clasped hands to her chest like she never wanted to forget the moment.

He tried to get comfortable on the wooden bench. Love at first sight didn't exist. First, friendship occurred. Mutual interests came next. Lots of chats followed. A few arguments could've happened to keep it real. The two of them plunged into their marriage without much more than a conversation.

"Was it something at first sight?" Pierce refused to use the word "love." Story finished, they both stood back up. He scooted around a college-age couple who held hands and smiled at each other as though no one else existed.

She tilted her head as they headed back to the sidewalk. "You could call it interest. He enthralled me right away when he said he planned to enroll in college."

When his cousin spotted Kendra, Pierce guessed he had probably viewed her as a living lifesaver. He should tell her now about David's lifelong struggle with his explosive temper that emerged as soon as someone became close to him. His cousin's efforts to push others away whenever anyone cared about him always worked. David had bulldozed anyone he needed to achieve this goal.

"He wanted to go to college?" David never had any interest in college before. Maybe Pierce made the mistake. It wasn't that Kendra didn't know David. No, he didn't know his cousin. He figured he understood everything about David. After all, he worked as a high school counselor. Comprehending others' feelings and their actions allowed him to perform his job well.

"Only athletics and riding his Harley interested him," Pierce said. Nothing else.

"There's that invisible motorcycle vrooming around us again. He said he wished he hadn't messed up in high school. He liked setting up the new sporting goods stores. His goal included management."

Pierce's chest tightened. "People change." That could include his cousin. "I hadn't seen him for a while. He never answered my texts. Ignored my emails. I didn't know where to send a letter. I gave up." And let everyone down. "I should've tried harder." Didn't family matter more than anything?

She stopped her meander past the town storefronts and turned to face him. Kendra's hand rested a moment on his forearm. Her touch equaled the breeze's gentleness.

"If you encouraged him and he pushed you away, that was his mistake, not yours."

Her words made that throb between his shoulder blades lessen a notch. "I tried to be the big brother he never had. I failed." The truth brought back his headache. The discomfort at his temples raged. They ended up next to a white-painted gazebo at the edge of Shallow Stream Park. In a little while, the dog Frisbee contest would begin.

"I'm not sure you failed. He turned out to be…"

"Mr. Mic!" two guys called out from the far side of the park.

He sucked in a gulp of air. Of all of his students who would raise a ruckus about Kendra, these were the two who'd win the award.

Kendra looked up at him. "I hope me being here with you won't start gossip."

"They'll know you're not my sister. It's a half-block before my students pounce and the questions begin." But he underestimated how quickly the two teens moved when inspired because they had spotted him with a pretty woman at his side. Like bloodhounds, they arrived, ready to sniff out the story.

"Mr. Mic, miss us?" Jake, a rising senior asked. He waggled his eyebrows.

"Meet Jake and Cort," Pierce answered, careful not to reveal their last names. "Are you enrolled in the summer math review?" Anything related to academics would make them stop staring at Kendra. He hoped. If he didn't take control, the town rumor mill would have him and Kendra engaged and picking out wedding bands before the festival ended.

"Nah, it's summer, man," Cort said. "No classes. Time to win volleyball games. Hang out at the lake. Take a break from school stuff. No offense, Mr. Mic."

Mr. McFarland, he wanted to say for at least the thousandth time. With Kendra at his side, he didn't bother. "None taken." They might be surprised to know he enjoyed a run around the lake and a pick-up volleyball game.

"It's time to chill." Cort took a step forward and smiled. He gave a nod and thumbs up, their secret code when they passed each other in the school hallway, meaning Cort's life didn't spiral out of control. "Who's the pretty woman?"

It figured that Cort doled out the first question. Before Pierce had a chance to answer, Kendra spoke up.

"An out-of-state visitor here to see family. I'm Kendra, Kendra McFarland."

She said her last name slowly and loudly so no one could possibly mistake it for any other name. Cort's shoulders slumped. His hot-off-the-presses story about how he caught his counselor with a beautiful woman deflated, then died.

Pierce held back a smile. "Nice to see you boys. Read this summer. Our public library awaits you. I told the librarian to be on the lookout for you both."

Cort and Jake's mouths fell open. "We gotta go."

"Do you think he really...?"Cort asked Jake as they turned and walked away.

Victory achieved, thanks to Kendra. He gave her an admiring glance. She knew the right thing to say.

"How'd you do that?" he asked.

"Do what?" She strode toward the fresh lemonade stand like a woman on a mission.

"Shut him down while being polite. I'm impressed. It takes teachers a while to learn that skill."

"Library circulation supervisors have tricks too," she said with one eyebrow raised. "I'm awestruck by you too. You knew them both well, I could tell. I bet they appreciate you taking the time to learn their names."

"I try. We communicate better if I know a little about them." He recalled the serious family issues both boys faced and wished he could do more.

She pushed away a tendril of hair. "Something wrong?"

"That's my line," he said. "It's hard not to think about their challenges."

"You try to fix everything for everyone."

The phrase she didn't say hung unspoken in the air. "I've made a lifetime habit of doing that." Apparently, he hadn't always done the best job. David's life might've been better without him hovering. Instead of saying anything else, he stepped up to the lemonade stand and ordered two large cups of the frosty drink.

She put her hands on her hips. "Brutal honesty here. Do you believe I'm pregnant?"

After he handed her the lemonade, a sip of the drink sloshed across her brightly colored sandals. No question could have surprised him more. The tang of the lemonade burned his throat and needed sweetening. "I believe you one hundred percent."

She put one hand on her waist. "Why can't I tell your aunt the truth about the exciting news?"

Wait. Honesty mattered. Lying? Had he asked her to lie? He stepped backward, and he almost tripped himself on the street's curb. "We're not telling her about the baby yet. My aunt, well, she hasn't done well these past few weeks. We need to break it to her slowly."

Her eyes widened. "So we say what? I'm a little bit pregnant? I'll start to show soon. The library where I work will be closed for a while. I planned to stay here. Your aunt said…it doesn't matter now. I'll stay somewhere else for that time. I'll figure it out."

Where?

Before Kendra and Aunt Meryl's disastrous meeting, "somewhere" meant the farmhouse, so she could live rent-free and locate that hidden money. Pierce took a breath that filled his lungs until they edged toward bursting. No way would he break his final promise to his cousin that he'd take care of his aunt. He'd never let his family down again. Keeping Kendra at the farmhouse would accomplish that. As much as he wanted to get to know this sweet, funny, and spirited woman better, he owed it to his family to do the right thing.

If he could keep Kendra away from his aunt for the day, he could get her to leave on good terms. If the day went well, he could promise her he'd search everywhere in the farmhouse for this supposed money his cousin had left behind. If only he could get her to trust him enough to agree. And he'd do it. He'd find her money. She deserved that much, and she'd agree to leave. His head stopped pounding quite as hard as he unraveled his plan. He needed to get through one single day. Then he'd get Kendra back on the road to Milwaukee, back to where she belonged. Away from him and his aunt, whom he'd vowed to protect.

Chapter Five

In front of the Juniper Juice stand with Pierce at her side, Kendra gulped the freshly squeezed lemonade and savored the sweet and sour mixed together. Like life, she decided. The image of Meryl McFarland burst uninvited into her musings. The woman despised her, and she had no clue as to why. Had Kendra insulted the woman somehow during the email exchange? Maybe ending each email with a smiley emoji caused Mrs. McFarland to believe Kendra hadn't been devastated by David's death. Despite their unresolved marital differences, it had only been the in the past week that she didn't awake with eyelids heavy with tears.

Had anyone in her life ever straightened and stiffened at her presence like Mrs. McFarland? Throughout elementary school, she often received the title "teacher's pet," much to the annoyance of her friends and to her own surprise. As a teenager, she'd been the one whom neighbors clamored to have babysit their children. Yet, Meryl McFarland wanted her out of her house, out of the state, and most of all, out of her life. In her few email responses, the woman seemed a person of sparse words. Nothing prepared her for meeting Mrs. McFarland. The woman was colder than the Wilson Ice Skating Arena, where Kendra spent many Saturday afternoons during high school falling across the ice.

Throughout their email exchange, Mrs. McFarland never questioned if Kendra had been married to her son. Kendra didn't want to ruin the day thinking about why Mrs. McFarland disliked her so much. Instead, she concentrated on the warm June breeze that tugged her French braid and sent loose tendrils flying. Even more, squinting through the sunshine she smiled at the kind gentleman who stared back at her without spitting out terrible names. What a welcome change from her late husband's abusive behavior.

"Want to see what made me semi-famous at Shorewood High School? C'mon." She reached out to take his hand. His strong grip warmed her as much as the sun's heat. She guided him through the crowd that swallowed them both like a storm surge. "People must come from all over to enjoy this fair. More people visit this festival than in your entire town, right?"

"You guessed right." Although he stood behind her, the smile in his voice came through.

When she reached the carnival games, a rainbow of stuffed animals peered back at them.

Her biceps tensed like the moments before she'd played softball. "Tell me what kind of toy I should win for the baby." The half-knitted baby's blanket she had crafted in the softest yarn she could find in mint green and white remained the only item she'd prepared for her unborn child. She leaned in closer and inspected the toys. "Second thought, I'm not sure these are baby-safe. Their eyes could fall out. Know an older child who loves stuffed animals?"

"My two nieces like nothing more. So this is your high school claim to fame, going to fairs and winning prizes?"

His puzzled look made her chuckle.

"I played softball and basketball throughout high school. I still play on a women's league for both sports." It sounded conceited. She sure didn't want him to think that. "I'm a terrible ice skater." For now, she'd continue to play sports. She'd need to clear her sports participation at her next doctor's appointment. If Dr. Engel hesitated even for a moment, she'd retire her baseball glove and basketball.

"I'd never have guessed you're practically a pro sports player. You're full of surprises."

Pleasant surprises, she hoped. Otherwise, the next two months during her stay in Shallow Stream would drag by. "Will you let me play until I win a toy for each of your nieces?"

"With your credentials, in another three minutes or so we'll be on our way. Then we can head to lunch."

His expression turned so serious, she wished for a hint about the lunchtime conversation topic. The smile he wore throughout the morning disappeared.

"How about fifteen minutes or less for me to win your nieces stuffed animals? That'll be my goal."

"Deal."

She rolled back her shoulders and stretched each arm.

The ball rested in her hand, smaller than a softball, but the familiar feeling caused her muscles to spark. Would her child someday play the sports she enjoyed? She imagined being at the park and giving her child the "pinkies and thumbs" tip.

"There's a line forming," the teenager behind the game counter said.

"Ready." She reared back in her pitcher mode. Strength sizzled up her arm. Without warning, the names David called her popped into her head. "Stupid." The word stung like a boxer's punch. Why now? Kendra blinked. She clutched the ball harder.

She circled in on the fluffy tiger with whiskers that looked like they'd tickle a child's plump cheeks.

Then, she inserted a word to replace stupid. He called her "stupid" a lot. That word ranked as one of his favorites, sometimes with an expletive or two tossed in. "You are so stupid, I've never known anyone so dumb," he'd shout with his eyes narrowed. No, she hadn't yet graduated from college, and she panicked at anything that required high-level math. She bit her lip hard. Still, smart described her. She let the ball go with a zing.

Bam.

"Whoa, I don't want to be in the batting cage and face you. Was that the one you wanted?" Pierce asked.

She nodded, glad that she hadn't overstated her abilities.

"Beginner's luck," the guy behind the counter grumbled before he tossed her the stuffed animal. "See it all the time. Bet you can't do it again."

Ignoring him, she turned to Pierce. "Which one should I try next?" She made sure to include "try." No guarantee she'd win another one. He did mention he had two nieces. She couldn't give only one child a prize.

"Hurry up," the worker said. "Others want to play."

A small group clustered to watch her. One little girl stood so close, Kendra moved forward so she'd have enough room for the wind-up pitch. She closed her eyes. Focused. Spectators had never bothered her before when she played sports. Out on the basketball court or baseball diamond, the crowds faded. This wouldn't be any different.

Kendra stared at her target and prepared for the next pitch. Kind and caring, she affirmed. Self-centered? No. That one was so far removed from the truth it almost made her chortle. That false label disappeared when she released the pitch.

Pow. Nailed it.

Lightness entered her chest and pushed away a corner of darkness. Sticks and stones might not break bones, but name calling from someone who claimed to love her broke her spirit. Now she needed to grab her confidence back. God's everlasting love would help her with that mission.

Pierce clapped, his grin returning. "You have one for each niece now."

"Two more tries, and I'll quit. Promise."

"You don't give up easily." Admiration filled his eyes. She smiled back and saw the pride when he looked at her. Renewed strength surged through her. She could do this, and he believed she could.

"Worthwhile" replaced "worthless." The new word floated. Right as she released the ball, the worker behind the counter coughed, pushing her off balance and breaking her concentration. The ball petered to the side and tumbled to the grass.

"No fair," someone from the group behind her called.

"Give her another chance," someone else said.

The worker's eyes bulged. "When you have to cough, you cough."

"Give her a free chance, or none of us will play."

Worthwhile, worthwhile, worthwhile, she chanted silently. *Please God,* she prayed, *let my heart believe my worth.*

In her damp hand, she squeezed the ball so hard the veins on her inner arm appeared. No man would ever talk to her like that again. She wouldn't let it happen.

Worthwhile.

The next two stuffed animals she scored with bulls' eyes. No chance she wouldn't win.

"Can you play for me?" The close-by little girl with pigtails pulled on Kendra's shirt.

"No," the worker barked. "Is your goal here to put me and my dad out of business? We have to buy these stuffed things, you know. No one gives them to us for free."

"I'll take the hint," Kendra said.

He waved them away and suggested they try another game. Pierce clutched the stuffed tiger, a frog, and a purple rabbit with pink ears.

She readjusted the butter-colored llama with a gold saddle and positioned it on her hip. A wave of fatigue washed over her.

"Let's get these into the Jeep and head off for lunch," he said.

"You're probably hungry. As usual, I'm famished. Wait. There's a craft section up there to the right," she said, after she lined up the toys into his Jeep's back seat. She pointed toward the corner of an open tent with tables set up and grabbed his arm. "I'll warn you, I could spend the whole day looking at crafts and figuring out how to replicate them."

From where she stood, she spotted a teal door wreath festooned with white-pearl beads. Kendra knew it would be the perfect birthday gift for Mrs. Syed, her landlord. A shiver danced up her spine as she pictured her neighbor's delight. She spotted a shawl her best friend would like. Her boss at the library would like that shawl, too, but in hunter green, her supervisor's favorite color.

"You do a lot of crafts?" he asked.

"Remember the scarf, hat, and mittens I knitted for your aunt?" As soon as she said the words, she wanted to take them back. No need to remind him of how much his aunt disliked her. "Knitting relaxes me. I forgot. From what I've seen, whenever you want to stay calm, you become the super baker and meal maker. I love reading the Bible and knitting when I feel stressed." She could've knitted a whole sweater to try to get Mrs. McFarland to stop her scowl. Too bad she left her knitting needles and yarn stashed at home.

He raised his eyebrows. "You seem content here."

At the library where she worked, her coworkers nicknamed her "Sunshine." "I am usually. But lately…" She shrugged as they passed the homemade pet treat table. She paused, lingering at the dog treats. Unfortunately, she didn't need anything from that table. David had refused to let her adopt from her landlord's puggle puppies in the downstairs apartment.

"A puppy? Seriously? You are crazy, certifiable," he had said as her shoulders had slumped at his words.

A newborn baby and a young pup wouldn't have been the best combination. Agreed. When things settled, she'd adopt a puppy from the Milwaukee animal shelter near her apartment. "I pray when I'm stressed. You should try it again. It really works."

"That's your secret?" He stopped walking.

"Pretty much. Oh, and I vacuum and eat carrots sometimes when I'm worried, while praying."

"No chocolate?" He put one hand over his heart. "I, Pierce Harland McFarland, am a chocoholic. I hide candy from myself to keep from eating it in one gulp."

Tears of joy streamed down her cheeks and moistened her collar. "Hah. Harland McFarland? You made that up. If not, don't let your students know. They'd never let you live it down."

"You caught me. Guilty as charged. I wanted to hear you laugh. And James, that's my middle name."

Turning toward the craft tables on her left, she had to change the topic of conversation fast. If he commented about her late husband's middle name, she'd shrug. Once again, something she didn't know. Their marriage certificate didn't list his middle name. Did he have one?

The crowd milled around them. A woman pushed her son in a stroller, her husband at her side. Leaning across the stroller, the woman rearranged the folds of the blanket over her baby. The wheels of the stroller clacked along the brick sidewalk. Kendra's heart skipped a beat at the ordinary, yet loving scene.

In front of the first craft table, she scrubbed her hands with the sanitizer. Then she rubbed her fingertips across a cream-colored shawl.

"Beautiful work," she said to the Black woman about her age who manned the table.

"Thanks, I made these, and you picked my favorite," the woman said. "Good eye."

"Like it?" Pierce reached into his pocket for his wallet.

She stared at him, open-mouthed. He hadn't hesitated to treat her, but he barely knew her. When she spotted the price, she pushed the item away. Kendra couldn't let him spend this kind of money on her.

Her cheeks heated. "I want to see how I could make it myself. Sorry, I know you're here to sell so that's not fair, but I won't buy anything today. I admire your beautiful work."

"A fellow knitter, I'll tell you a secret. That's the real reason I'm here." The woman leaned forward, and her dark eyes gleamed. "I want to connect with other knitters. We have a knitting club and meet at the community center on Pine Avenue at 7p.m. Wednesday nights, if you're interested. We'd love to grow our group." She scribbled her name, cell phone number, and email on a scratch piece of paper.

"Nice to meet you, Meg. I plan to be here for a few months. Maybe I'll stick around longer." How fun it would've been to have a friend who loved to knit. Joining a knitting club ranked high on her to-do list. She could never find one that worked with her schedule in Milwaukee.

"If you want to attend, you're more than welcome to stop by whenever you can. Both of you can join. We have couples and men who come to knit." Meg smiled.

"I don't knit. I have no plans to start." Pierce frowned.

"You don't know what you're missing." A pair of intricate baby booties caught Kendra's eye. Putting her hands behind her back, she kept herself from checking out the stitches. She folded the paper with Meg's contact information and slid it into her purse's side pocket. Zipping the pocket closed, she said to him, "Let me know when you can't stand any more crafts. I could linger here all day."

A crowd of people surged around them, and she stepped closer to him. Yes, she'd like to get to know Pierce better. After all, he was her relative, so that was to be expected. Pierce made her laugh. When she spoke, he leaned toward her and looked into her eyes as though she said something worthwhile. With his long stride, wide shoulders, and eyes that drew her close, even a glance at him made her breath catch. Nothing wrong with wanting to know a cousin. That is, if she could hang around him without his aunt glaring at her. His deep voice made her body relax. That easy smile of his caused her to smile back. Other than the day she received the pregnancy news, she couldn't remember the last time she grinned so much that her cheeks ached. How had she forgotten about this small pleasure?

Kendra glanced back at the table's knitted items of hats and shawls. She peered around his broad shoulders.

"See what I see?" She smiled.

"More crafts. I want to treat you to that lunch. There's something I need to talk to you about." That forehead frown of his returned. Whatever bad news he wanted to share could wait.

"But I love the Ferris wheel," she said, as they strolled back toward the car, not caring that she sounded like a five-year-old. Who didn't love Ferris wheels? Besides, she could view the whole town from the top of the Ferris wheel and pick out the places she wanted to explore.

"Hmm, how should I say this? It isn't safe for a pregnant woman who is my guest, who happens to be you."

"The drive here was at a higher speed than the Ferris wheel," she said.

"It's not a great idea. Let's go to lunch. Afterward, we can discuss it. Does that sound like a fair compromise?"

She nodded, shocked that he hadn't made the decision, even though he presented his stance. "I like compromises." She hadn't experienced many.

Although he nodded, those forehead frown lines remained. He planned to serve something up at lunch besides pizza, and whatever his menu, it wouldn't be palatable.

Chapter Six

The scent of Dimorio's cheese, pizza dough, and sausage made Pierce's mouth water as he stepped into the restaurant. Even more, memories grabbed him by the throat and shook him. The same red velvet curtains from his high school days hung in the window. The always-blue arch that led into the eating area had recently been painted over white, though. Even at Dimorio's some things changed. Positioned close to the front door, the jukebox rolled out tunes. He wanted to grasp Kendra's hand and twirl her in beat to the music.

Before she relaxed in the booth, Kendra spouted off her order to the waiter who walked beside them. "Hi, I'd like to order a pepperoni pizza, extra pepperoni with onion and green peppers, oh and some artichokes. Thanks so much."

"A single piece of pizza?" the waiter asked, not writing a word of it on his green order pad.

"No, a small pizza would be good. Second thought, let's make that a medium." She paused.

Pierce anticipated her next words.

"A large pizza would be best. I might have some leftovers for later in case I get hungry in the middle of the night."

The night she planned to sleep at the farmhouse again. Tucked into the guestroom bed, maybe the next morning she could eat the breakfast he prepared. The night he hoped she'd head home on I-94 back to Milwaukee.

"A whole large pizza just for you?" the waiter asked. "Or is that for the two of you to share?"

"Yes, all for me. I'm famished. Plus, I'd like a large glass of ice water with lemon slices, please. Oh, and a large green salad, too, please. Thanks so much."

"I'll have the pizza combo with the deluxe salad," Pierce said. "The food tastes great here. The owner is a former vet, so the town tries hard to support him with their business." He glanced around, and, for the first time, noticed the sun had bleached the edges of the red curtains. "The place could use some updates. We don't notice it until we see it through someone else's eyes." The casual surroundings didn't seem to bother her.

"You hung out with David here?"

He pointed. "Right there in that booth." Those Friday nights he acted as babysitter, never taking his eyes off his mischievous cousin. How would Pierce have spent his free time during high school if he hadn't volunteered to make sure his cousin stayed out of trouble? Track team and cross-country ranked as possibilities.

"This place seems great. How could your aunt ask so much of a high school kid? Did you ever have fun?"

Not much, not any fun. At the fair, he remembered how good it felt to be out in the sun and enjoy a day. "I didn't have to agree to help out my aunt. My uncle had recently died of liver cancer. Once I said yes, I couldn't let her down. It became my mission. Save David." Save David from himself. Now the same went for his aunt. He had a new mission, no matter how much he wanted to reject the promise. Aunt Meryl wouldn't get better with her daughter-in-law not only in town but also camped out at the farmhouse. Kendra planned to stick around. Hadn't she told Meg months? His aunt couldn't have possibly agreed to that arrangement. Even if she did, in her current state his aunt would only worsen, aggravated by Kendra's presence.

Pierce fiddled with his napkin. "I'm glad we shared this day. You'll have to reveal your secrets to winning those stuffed animals. My nieces will expect me to do that next summer."

"Practice, lots and lots of practice pitching," she said. "I've had a lot of fun today too. Thank you."

Her eyes sparkled. How could he possibly ask her to leave when she wanted to stay? He sensed she hadn't gotten much of what she wanted in life. Plus, he wanted to hear her laugh. Her enthusiasm and positive outlook were contagious. Even, to his shock, her earlier prayer made the knots in his neck dissolve.

Could he reach his hand across the restaurant's Formica table and grasp her fingers in his? Tell her how much he enjoyed her company. Pull her soft hand closer. Still, that promise lingered like a raincloud ready to burst. How could he go back on his word to his late cousin? What would happen to his aunt if he did?

The waiter brought their food. When she lowered her head in prayer, he followed suit. This time, he didn't require prodding. Then he cleared his throat. He couldn't delay what he needed to say any longer. Pierce wanted each word to sound as kind as possible. She deserved that and more. "If you want to go home now and get back to your job, I'll scour the house. That money? I'll find it for you. It's no problem. My aunt won't notice me nosing around. You search through the house? That's a different story." Aunt Meryl would add it to her growing list of reasons she disliked Kendra.

The light dimmed as if an eclipse passed over her eyes. He shifted in his seat. The booth's leather stuck against his khakis and held him in place. "I have no use for the money. Trust me."

"That's what David wrote," Kendra said, her voice flat. "I believe you. Why wouldn't I?"

To his relief, she didn't add, "Besides, we're family."

"I promise I'll give you every cent." More promises that he needed to keep. He would, too. He certainly wouldn't steal money David had worked hard to earn for her. She and the baby would need those funds. She stared at him now, no ready smile, no sparkling eyes, and no tears. Why wasn't she fighting back? Anger sputtering from her would make the conversation easier. She remained silent.

"You probably want to return to Milwaukee, to your friends, to your life." He left his aunt out of it. Wanting it to sound positive rather than negative. After all, Kendra was the positivity queen, overflowing with prayer and her faith.

"I hoped," she began, studying the half-filled plate of pizza before her. "I hoped I'd find family here. That's what I want more than anything, for me and the baby."

Aunt Meryl would be as likely to claim Kendra as family as a mouse would adopt a rattlesnake.

He started shredding the napkin's second corner. "I'll stay in contact. We can email, text, call. I'll visit you. Milwaukee isn't far away." The back of his neck throbbed. How could he do this? By the abandoned look on her face, he assumed he'd never see her again. Not if she had anything to say about it. What about what he wanted? Her gone from his life made emptiness stretch before him like the endless cornfields off the interstate.

"That's not necessary for you to text. I don't like email much anymore."

Thanks to Aunt Meryl.

She suddenly found the tabletop to be captivating. And he couldn't blame her. No matter how he said the words, he'd still asked her to leave.

"I understand," she said and picked at her pizza crust.

They both remained silent for the rest of the meal.

"Guess my eyes were bigger than my stomach," Kendra said, when the waiter came back to wrap up the rest of her pizza.

"I don't know about that. You ate more than the average football player, and you finished your salad like a champ," the waiter said.

"Thanks." She gave a small smile.

David waited for her to say the waiter insulted her regarding how much she ate. Lacey would've jumped to her high heels and demand to speak to the restaurant owner. Then again, his ex-fiancée had never agreed to step foot into "that dump."

Kendra's face turned as pale as the napkin she held. She bent forward and clutched her stomach.

"What's wrong?" He rushed from his side of the booth and knelt beside her.

"I don't know…I…need…to go to the hospital. " Pain creased her face. "Now."

Chapter Seven

Pierce revved up the Jeep as Kendra's insides squeezed like a boa constrictor had wrapped within her belly and wouldn't let go. Nothing bad could happen to this baby. She remained responsible for this life growing inside her. Had she done something wrong? If so, she couldn't live with that truth. At least at Pierce's insistence, they had skipped the Ferris wheel. Was this pain that jabbed her belly happening because David didn't want this baby?

Pierce overshot the speed limits by twenty miles per hour.

"Drive faster," she said.

Each time the Jeep hit a pothole, she cringed and prayed the baby hadn't been jostled. If pulled over by the police, all the better. They could use a police escort to arrive quicker. The ten-minute drive to Mercy Hospital at the edge of Shallow Stream seemed to take as long as her journey from Milwaukee. She placed her hands protectively over her stomach.

"Please, God, keep this baby safe."

"Amen," Pierce said.

An ER attendant greeted them in the parking lot with a wheelchair that squeaked as he helped her into the chair.

"What's your name?" he asked.

"Kendra Hester."

"Kendra McFarland," Pierce said at the same time. "She's pregnant."

"Are you the father?" the attendant asked, as he rolled the wheelchair toward the Emergency Room.

"No, but I'm family."

The word echoed in her ears. Never had she wanted more to hear that word spoken aloud. She wanted to grab it and wrap it around her belly like a blanket keeping her baby warm. The parking lot pebbles that clinked against the wheelchair seemed the size of boulders.

"For now, please stay in the waiting room, sir," the attendant said. "We'll give you an update soon. Our examination rooms are small."

"Please, let him come with me," she blurted. Minutes earlier, this man had asked her to leave the farmhouse. Leave the state. Although he said the words with gentleness, it didn't change the truth. He wanted her gone today and forever. Her throat caught. Why then, did she want him to stay? Why did she want him in the examination room with her, standing by her side, holding her hand, and supporting her?

He gave her hand one last squeeze. His strength and good wishes traveled up her arm and nestled into her heart.

"I'll be right here in the waiting room. I'm not going anywhere. I promise. Plus, I'll keep positive thoughts until they come out and tell me you and the baby are fine."

Prayers, she wanted more prayers that were like nourishment for her and her unborn child.

Tears filled her eyes. "Thank you."

Yes, she wanted him with her as he murmured words of reassurance. That seemed to be too much to ask.

"He'll be close by. After the doctor has a better idea of what's going on, we'll let him know," the attendant said.

Her abdomen contracted. The attendant rushed her from the hospital parking lot toward the hospital entrance. The Emergency Room doors that appeared so far in the distance finally flung open with a whoosh.

Waving goodbye, he leaned forward like he planned to kiss her cheek, then as his check grazed hers, he pulled back.

A new ache pushed through her belly. Oh no, she couldn't be in labor, could she? No way would the baby survive being born this early. "God, please provide love and safety to this little one. Let everything be okay for this innocent baby." Never had she prayed so hard that God would hear her heartfelt words and answer her prayer. She squeezed her clasped hands together as though nothing could ever pull her hands apart.

"Anything unusual happen today?" the attendant asked. Concern flooded his face.

The entire day flashed before her, starting with how Pierce made her breakfast. Mostly, she pictured Pierce as he smiled and joked. The way his eyes twinkled when he glanced her way. During their late lunch she wanted to sink under the table after he had requested she leave. That appeal came out of nowhere. She thought he liked her as much as she liked him. She had sure read him wrong.

"I don't think I overdid it earlier today." Maybe Pierce had been right getting them to leave when they did. "I ate some spicy food. That pepperoni pizza was the best I've ever tasted. I can't imagine that scrumptious food caused this pain."

"Dimorio's?" the attendant asked. He eased her into the hospital bed.

"Been there?"

"It's my favorite. I love the crust, and the pepperoni can't be beat."

"Let's see what's going on here," a nurse said as she entered the examining room. "After I ask you some questions and do a quick initial exam, the doctor will talk to you. Can you give me the name and number of your physician?"

She told the nurse her doctor's name. Then her stomach cramped again. She brought her knees forward and clenched her fists. "This hurts." Wouldn't actual labor hurt more? Was this a test? Because David didn't want the baby, did that mean she'd have complications, or worse? What if…She couldn't let herself finish that sentence.

A second nurse came by minutes later. "The doctor has ordered another test," he said.

"Another one? Does that mean the doctor thinks something is wrong?" Kendra asked.

"No," the nurse answered. "The doctor wants to be very thorough. He's reviewing your medical files and has already contacted your OB/GYN in Milwaukee. We checked, and everything is covered by your insurance. Try to relax and rest. Know you are in the best possible place right now."

She nodded. "I'll do whatever they tell me to do to keep this baby safe." Her hands shook. How could she have been so careless to eat anything that might make her feel unwell? Maybe her late husband had been right when he called her "stupid."

"I doubt you did a single thing wrong. Worrying won't help. See if you can close your eyes. Sleep would be the best for you."

Sleep? She'd never been more awake with worry, although Pierce's positive thoughts helped. She should've asked him to pray when he stood at her side. Around her, machines beeped. The smell of antiseptic made her nose itch. From the hallway, orderlies guided patients on gurneys with clacking wheels that whirred past the room's open door. They maneuvered the gurneys through the hallways or into examining rooms.

Two hours and three tests later, the doctor returned with the results. Smiling, he went over each test and paused twice to ask if she had any questions.

"Thank you, doctor. Could someone please get Pierce McFarland from the waiting room? He's been here all this time." *For me*, she nearly added, still astounded he'd wait for her. "He's a good friend."

"I'll get someone to bring him back. Now, remember my instructions."

"I will," Kendra said. She smoothed the blanket under her chin and the heat flooded her chest and her breaths quieted. "I'll do whatever I need to do to have a healthy baby."

"That's the kind of talk every doctor wants to hear." He looked over his shoulder. "You must be Pierce. I'll give you two a few minutes. Then I'll be back to see if there are any questions." He left the room.

"Hi," Pierce said. Pulling up the chair next to the bed, he grasped her hand. Her breathing softened at his touch.

"You waited all this time. Thank you. Everything is fine," she said, before he had a chance to worry one more minute. "The doctor wants me to rest more and avoid stress and ah...spicy food. Nothing I did caused this, except that maybe I had the world's worst case of indigestion. The details of my stomach distress you probably could live without hearing. They ran tests. The baby is fine, and that's all that matters."

He cleared the strands of hair off her cheek, and she warmed under his touch. "You're okay too. That also matters. I'm glad to hear you and the baby are fine. I'll move your things into the cottage today before you get home. You'll have privacy and a quiet environment."

She released the blankets she hadn't even known she fisted. "Where will you go?" She guessed the cottage had a couch, but the last thing he needed was to do anything that started the rumors bubbling.

Pierce helped her out of bed. "I rent an apartment near the high school. The tenant remains in my apartment still, but he should've already moved out. I'll go there soon. Or I can sleep in the cottage's second bedroom tonight."

"That's a good idea," the doctor said, entering the room. "You need someone close by. I'm glad to see you are dressed and ready to leave the hospital. Let me reiterate the importance of getting help once you arrive home."

Home would be her Milwaukee apartment in a two-flat building, and she knew the doctor didn't mean she should immediately travel to Wisconsin. "But you said..."

"Everything's fine. I also said you need rest and fluids. He can make sure that happens." The doctor nodded toward Pierce. "I wanted someone with you when I share some additional news."

The doctor paused. Concern flickered across Pierce's face.

"You said nothing's wrong." Kendra sat up too fast. Around her, the room blurred. Tears flooded her eyes like a dam about to burst. "You shouldn't have additional news."

"Nothing *is* wrong," the doctor said. He placed a hand on her shoulder and gave a squeeze. "Take a deep breath. This is good news. The nurse heard two strong heartbeats, as did I."

Kendra gasped.

"Sometimes, it can be an echo. In your case, let me be the first to offer you congratulations on your twins."

She fell back against the pillow that offered a cloud's softness. "Twins. I'm being blessed with two babies?" Tears trickled across her lips. But it also meant double the expenses and the worries. She took another deep breath. God would hear her prayers often.

"Twins," the doctor repeated. "Everything looks good. You need to get extra rest, throughout the pregnancy, but especially right now."

"Thank you, doctor," Pierce said. "I'm relieved everything is okay with both Kendra and her baby." He smiled. "Sorry, babies. That will take getting used to."

"You said earlier how tough it would be for me to have twins." The words came out like an accusation, which she didn't mean.

"I didn't know you were having twins then. I meant in general. Ignore me. I know nothing about babies, only high school students. Give me fifteen years, and I can provide decent advice."

"Let's talk a moment," the doctor said, motioning for Pierce to follow him and head halfway down the hallway. The twins were her babies to love and take care of. What could the doctor possibly want to discuss with Pierce that didn't include her? She bit her lip. Her razor-sharp hearing captured the doctor's every word.

"I meant what I said about her needing to reduce stress. I understand her husband recently died. Can anyone make sure she relaxes more? I'd like her to stay in bed for the next forty-eight hours at least. I'd keep her here at the hospital so that we could watch her, but I don't have any viable reason to do so. I don't want her to end up with a medical bill not covered by insurance."

More than ever, she needed to find the money her late husband hid for her somewhere in that farmhouse. Where could it be, and how could she ever locate the funds now?

"I'll watch over her," Pierce said. "No one will bother her."

She knew exactly who Pierce meant.

"She seems strong after her husband's death. Sometimes, patients are too sturdy at the onset of a tragedy and then have difficulties later. I'm not a psychiatrist by training, but I'm guessing that's what's happening. She needs support. She mentioned something about staying at her mother-in-law's farmhouse. Could her mother-in-law assist her?"

"Ah, that's not likely," Pierce said.

Kendra gave a sigh of relief.

~~~~~

Had Pierce's request for Kendra to leave resulted in this hospital visit? The clatter of gurneys and elevators binging made him so relieved he could watch her back home rather than leaving Kendra hospitalized. Every few minutes, announcements blared from the intercom. If he could keep her in the cottage he'd renovated last summer, she'd appreciate the robins' morning tweets and crickets' chirps throughout the night. She needed the rest and the calm the cottage always offered him. He hoped it would work for her too. Right now, Kendra's health and wellbeing outranked his aunt's grief.

"Everything really is okay, right? I mean, doctors need to take oaths," she said.

With his thumb, he dried the single tear that slid down her cheek. He wished he could keep his finger touching the softness of her face.

"I'm sorry I'm being such a baby. I try to not worry. Sometimes, that's hard, almost impossible. Sometimes I forget I'm not in control, but God always is," she said. "I need to keep reminding myself of that fact."

"It's okay, I promise. The doctor wanted to talk to me about you needing support. I'm here for you. I'll bring you straight to the cottage and then tote your things over. You overheard everything he said, right?" He wanted to wrap his arms around her and hug her close. Now was not the time.

"That doctor's booming voice isn't the best for secrets." She smiled. "Someone should tell him."

"Does your friend Alyssa that you mentioned work with you at the library? If so, you could contact her. She's welcome to stay at the cottage too. It would be good for you to have a friend right now." Did Kendra view him as a friend? Probably not after he tried to kick her out of the farmhouse and rush her back to Milwaukee.

"She works at the library, also furloughed, but she's taking some college courses this summer. She's halfway through her classwork, and I wouldn't want to cause trouble. What about your aunt? I know this sounds mean, it's her cottage and all, but maybe I don't need to see her right now."

"No worries. My aunt won't come near you. I have the only key to the cottage. I'll tell her what happened soon. She'll take it better from me." That was an understatement. "Once she knows about the pregnancy and the twins, she won't bother you. Let's get you out of here and go home."

Home, that was what Kendra needed. After what he'd done, would she ever call Shallow Stream home?

Chapter Eight

"The doctor believes Kendra never mourned when David died. Now she's experiencing those emotions," Pierce said. His aunt scowled at him from across the farmhouse's kitchen table.

As he stood up, he walked four steps to turn off the teakettle and added the boiled water to his aunt's waiting china cup, her favorite.

"Don't let it brew too long. I don't like my tea strong. She barely knew my son. How could she mourn him? That's the real problem." She tapped her fingernails on the kitchen table. "I bet she doesn't know the name of his best friend, his favorite color, or that he liked to eat cold spaghetti and pizza as his preferred breakfast. Then there's the motorcycle. Do you believe that David didn't share his love of motorcycles with his supposed wife? That bike meant everything to him. What happened? That's what I want to know."

It had been the most words his aunt had uttered since David's death. Even though her anger sputtered, she spoke in full sentences. A good sign. To his relief, she had washed and brushed her hair. Glimmers of Aunt Meryl's former self emerged.

He lifted the teabag out of the cup. "When did you see David last? People change."

"No one changes that much. I'm his mother, and mothers know these things." Aunt Meryl narrowed her eyes. "She's not his type. Not in looks or actions. All his girlfriends were petite, blonde-haired, and quiet."

Yes, and he didn't marry any of them. David had picked Kendra.

"Kendra is anything but quiet," his aunt said with a scowl. "Those young women let David take charge, which he liked. This one is nothing like them."

"Guaranteed Kendra wouldn't appreciate being referred to as 'this one.'" He stood back up from the kitchen table to avoid meeting his aunt's glare and tossed the tea bag into the trash. "For now, she'll stay at the cottage where she can relax."

His aunt straightened in her chair. "You'll be there too? What will people in the town think once they hear about that nonsense?"

He wouldn't share the details of his plan to be sure no one questioned Kendra's reputation. Pierce leaned against the table and peered into his aunt's already half-empty teacup. "I'll take care of everything. Want more tea?" he asked before he could stop the automatic words.

She waved him away. "Don't be so naïve. Everyone knows everything in this small town. This sort of thing always has a way of coming out. The gossip, the scandal, would be all over your high school in a second. Your career would be ruined."

Had she not heard him?

"I won't stay in the cottage. I don't want to invade Kendra's privacy."

Although his aunt overreacted, part of him believed some truth remained within her statement. As a tenured teacher with "excellent" performance appraisals, his career wouldn't be over. He tried to be a role model for students who didn't have anyone to look up to at home. Students like Cort. They watched him. Made sure his words and actions matched. The kids wouldn't care about the gossip, but he would. Plus, he didn't want anything to hurt Kendra's reputation, even if she never set foot in Shallow Stream again. She deserved better.

"I'll take care of it," Aunt Meryl said. "Take care of her, I mean, if she moves back into the guest room. I could watch over her."

It? Still a spark of his once-thoughtful aunt again appeared. The same woman who delivered her famous home-cooked lasagna to new moms and offered to babysit siblings to give those same moms a short break. The woman who volunteered in the nursery at church so parents could enjoy services without a wiggling baby.

Pierce had promised the doctor he'd reduce Kendra's stress and not create more. He wanted to remind his aunt that she could barely take care of herself. Hadn't he been the one doing that for her these past months?

"What about me?" she asked. "Who'll make my dinners? Or clean up around here if you're busy with that woman?"

All empathy for his aunt vanished. "She's not 'that woman.'" In his anger, he almost slipped and spilled the pregnancy news. "You could make your dinner yourself."

"I'm not feeling up to that type of responsibility on a daily basis. Besides, you're the better cook."

He raised his eyebrows at her attempt at humor. "True." Before the death of her son, Aunt Meryl's quick wit caused the family to laugh hard enough to cause stomachaches at the dinner table. Yet, her newfound independence lasted less than one minute.

"I'll call Jill. She can stay a few days. The kids just finished preschool and kindergarten. They'll see it as a vacation," he said.

Aunt Meryl's eyes widened at the idea of two squealing children, ages five and under, tearing through her farmhouse.

"That doesn't sound like a good solution. I'll need to put away all my glass knickknacks."

"I can't move back into my apartment, even though my tenant should've been gone by now." He glanced at the clock that hung over the archway entrance into the kitchen. "If you're worried about your breakable items, I'll position them in the curio before I check on Kendra."

"Thank you."

He took a step backward. Although he didn't need her gratitude, not once before had she thanked him.

"Keep away from that girl," she added.

Again, they'd circled back to where they had started. "That woman's name is Kendra." He wanted to add that she was the mother of his aunt's grandchild. Now was not the right time to disclose the truth only Kendra had the right to announce.

"I'm not convinced she knew him, much less married him. I want to see a marriage certificate. Then I'll believe her." His aunt's eyes blazed. "Maybe."

"Who carries around a marriage certificate?"

"Who sends an email or two and then shows up unwanted at someone's house?"

He raised his eyebrows. "I saw the multiple emails. You invited her." Busted. She had the same look on her face that his students had when they skipped class and he caught them pulling into the high school parking lot.

"There must be photos of the wedding ceremony. Those selfies everyone takes at least." She waved her hand. "What does Kendra really want from us? I want to know the answer to that question."

"She wants family," he said. She had looked in awe at the photos with all the McFarland family gathered together.

"That's not it."

With his back turned, he chuckled as he rinsed his aunt's teacup and placed it into the dishwasher. "You tell me then. I guess she's after the McFarland riches." Did his aunt know about the money left for Kendra? Now would be a perfect time for her to confess. He opened that door and hoped his aunt would stroll inside. He could turn over the money to Kendra and be relieved she left with at least one thing she needed.

"That could very well be," she said. "Is my laptop nearby?"

"In the office on the table where you left it." To his shock, she stood up and strode to the office instead of asking him to fetch the computer and set it up for her.

"I'm going to be busy. Knock on the office door if you need me," she said.

If he needed his aunt, that would be the first time ever in their relationship. "Sure. I'll check on Kendra."

"Yes, you do that." She stepped out of the office. "Once she starts to feel stronger, she can leave. That'd be best for everyone. I'm still too tired to handle a guest. I don't know why she pushed so hard for me to invite her. I never wanted her here."

"So, you finally admit that you did invite her."

His aunt's bottom lip quivered. "Yes, under duress, I did. Does she ever take a hint? I forgot about it because I never expected her to actually show up."

"You owe her an apology. I'll tell her if you don't. She's torn up about the ideas that none of the McFarland family welcomed her, and you think she arrived uninvited."" He closed the dishwasher with a thud. "I'll tell her when I feel comfortable doing so and with an apology."

That time had already passed. As much as he wanted to protest, he'd let her decide when to say sorry, as long as the apology occurred. He left her to her laptop and whatever Internet searches she planned.

After he left the farmhouse, Pierce jogged through the winding path that led to the cottage. His legs begged for a full-out run into town or on his favorite forest preserve trail that wove along the lake. That run would coax his muscles to burn, but it would mean leaving Kendra alone. Dusk already descended. He'd already been away too long.

Why did his aunt harbor so much suspicion? Was this part of the depression he guessed she'd endured? At this point, her behavior seemed more than grief.

Once outside, the summer air refreshed him. He checked his phone. A text from his sister Jill confirmed that she and her daughters would be by in the morning, delighted to enjoy an unexpected farm vacation. He hoped Jill warned her two daughters that their great-aunt no longer had the horses, sheep, and goats she once kept. After her son's death, Aunt Meryl had sold all the livestock. His sister wouldn't miss the goats that had terrified her as a child, after one nibbled on the edge of her T-shirt. Jill had howled she'd be eaten. The closest his nieces would get to an animal were the stuffed ones Kendra won before that disastrous lunch.

Thank you, he texted Jill back. *Looking forward to seeing all of you.*

Before he knew it, he stood at the cottage door, feeling like a visitor. He gave the front door knocker two loud taps before entering the cottage foyer.

"Kendra?"

"In here in the bedroom, snuggled under the covers," she said. "I'm following orders and resting."

He gave the bedroom door another knock before opening it. She sat propped up in bed, a trio of pillows stacked behind her. A bunch of inspirational romance novels sat on the dresser, and she clutched one.

"How's it going?"

"The reading? Great books. Thank you for letting me borrow them from your aunt. I hope she doesn't mind."

She would mind if she knew.

"I'm fine, except for feeling silly. I should've never had that pizza on top of everything else I ate. And I really overdid it today, especially when I started out feeling so queasy. That doctor told me I need to listen to my body more."

He squeezed her hand, and she rewarded him with that amazing smile of hers that warmed him to his toes.

"Do you think that's what caused the episode?" he asked. Pierce pulled the chair closer to the bed, and it squeaked across his hardwood floor.

She sat up higher in the pillows, and her hair fanned behind her.

"It's been tough. I won't lie. The doctor might be right that all of this is catching up to me now. With David, things were more difficult than I expected and nothing like when we dated."

The fan's whir filled the room. "Want to talk about it?" Those words often coaxed his students to confide whatever bothered them.

"I'm guessing you're a good listener. You probably hear about teen angst all the time, even though I'll be thirty-one on June twenty-fourth."

Would she still be in town by then? He'd remember her birthday. "Some of the student problems I listen to rank as serious. Thirty-two years ago, when I was born, things seemed much different. Easier somehow."

Kendra chuckled. "From what you said about your aunt asking you to watch over David during high school, I'm wondering if you didn't take time then to enjoy a regular high school experience."

He studied his hands. Kendra leaned forward, taking on his counselor role. It seemed strange to sit on "the other side of the desk." "Hey, isn't this my job? You could be right. To my aunt's credit, I could've told her no." Especially after hearing her confession that she had invited Kendra, Aunt Meryl ranked as the last subject he wanted to discuss. "Tell me about you."

"There's not much to tell. I always planned to be a teacher," she said.

"You too?"

"When I was little, I had a class of my stuffed animals. Clem the cat always ranked as the star student, even after he lost one of his googly eyes." She smiled at the memory. "I read to my stuffed animals all the time. As I grew older, I loved the idea of helping kids learn to relish reading. I wanted to be a reading specialist. We didn't have enough money for me to get a four-year degree, even though my mom said otherwise. A year before she died, she gave me two years' worth of college money. I could go back to school at any time or use the money elsewhere. And that's what I'll do."

He welcomed the news that she had some funds. He might not succeed at locating the hidden money. The farmhouse had been renovated throughout the years to a rambling, four-bedroom home that included hiding places. Her twins could be in kindergarten by the time he unearthed Kendra's hidden treasure.

"Loans? Grants?" He had this conversation with students all the time when he encouraged them to pursue college.

She waved her hand as if pushing away his words. "I didn't want debt. Anyway, I discovered I loved the library. When the children's librarian went on maternity leave, they asked me to do her Saturday morning story time. They paid me to come in and read to the children. Can you believe that? I enjoyed it even more than when I read to Clem as a child."

He pictured Kendra surrounded by a group of children leaning forward and captivated by her every word. She probably acted out all the parts and gave each character an individual voice.

"Then David came into the library," he said. "Surprised the building didn't collapse around him."

"Excuse me?"

"Nothing. You met him, he wanted a library card, and a couple of weeks later, you married." It seemed way too fast.

She frowned. "It didn't happen quite like that. We spent each day together to get to know one another. Although he didn't attend church with me like he promised."

No surprise.

"Never did he mention a motorcycle, only that he started over. He wanted stability before he left for overseas," she said.

His cousin wanted the back road motorcycle ride's fast speed, not stability. "You married him, just like that."

She snapped her fingers. "Yep, I know it sounds strange. He did everything right, or so I thought at the time. We talked about kids in a couple of years. I was so surprised when..."

"When what?" His counseling training threw him into high alert and made his muscles tense. What had his cousin said that hurt Kendra so deeply her face blanched at the mention of his name? If David had so much as laid a finger on her…

"Nothing. Would you mind if I rested a bit or maybe did some more reading?"

"Of course," he said. "Do you have your phone in case you need anything? I'll bring you a tray of food soon."

"I don't need a food tray. I know how to cook. I can fix my own dinner. If I've given you the impression I'm helpless, I'm not." She pushed up higher against her pillows, so she almost sat upright.

"The doctor stated you need to stay in bed for forty-eight-hours. It would make me happy to know that I helped your recovery."

"Fine, I have my phone right on the night table. Won't you be in the other bedroom?"

""I'll get you something to eat first."

A half-hour later, he brought her a tray with a green salad and a sliced apple.

"I'll bring you a full dinner later. "

"Thank you, this treat looks scrumptious," she said.

"Need anything else?"

"After I finish eating, I'll take a nap. Thanks again for the healthy snack."

"Of course. I'm going outside now. Do some yard work. Call me if you need anything."

As he stepped past the cottage's front porch, he hoped she'd take him up on that offer, and he'd hear his phone ring from her wanting his company.

Chapter Nine

As the afternoon melted into evening, Kendra considered her limited options for SOS calls, complete with flares. She wouldn't contact Alyssa. Her best friend would drop everything to rush to her side. Kendra only had to ask. That was the kind of friendship they had had since they met the first day of kindergarten and hugged by the end of class.

She'd do the same for Alyssa. Her friend had taken every overtime option at the library and worked a second job at The Edge coffee shop, down the street from Kendra's apartment. This all occurred while Alyssa took college classes. No way could her friend be an option.

If she knew Meg better, the knitter from the craft show, she could ask her for help, but she didn't. That left Pierce, the same man who showed her such kindness but also asked her to leave. Her throat ached at that memory. Another McFarland rejected her. The list grew.

Kendra hoped he'd been correct when he said his aunt didn't have a key to the cottage. It didn't rank as considerate, but the thought of facing Mrs. McFarland made Kendra's stomach churn. She had enough with stomach issues for the day and didn't welcome any more.

Early in the evening, Pierce announced his return to the cottage with a knock on her bedroom door. "I hope I didn't wake you. I'll head to the kitchen and make you some dinner."

Later, Pierce arrived back in the bedroom. With the dinner tray held high over his head, his biceps tensed beneath his T-shirt, and she couldn't look away.

"Voila!"

"Whoa, that's impressive. Don't drop the tray," she said.

"Never. I failed to mention that I worked at Dimorio's, part-time, too."

"You lived at that place." Although they had the best pizza she ever tasted, she couldn't imagine spending free time in high school at the restaurant the way he did. Playing sports like she did and being involved in her church's youth group seemed to be better options.

"I did such a terrible job of waiting tables that they put me on kitchen duty. That's where I learned to cook," he said.

She imagined them cooking together in the kitchen. Her having him taste-test as she held the spoon close to his mouth. Kendra pictured

Pierce's lips lingering near hers.

She bit her lip and concentrated on the meal set before her. "This looks delicious. No cheese or pizza in sight. Your dinner includes what I need—a light and healthy meal with lots of veggies. Thank you. Join me?"

"Never thought you'd ask. I'll grab another plate." When he returned, he perched at the chair beside her bed, ready to eat.

"This tastes as good as it looks." Kendra forced herself to take nibbles when she wanted to gulp the steamed salmon, broccoli, and carrots he prepared.

"How are you feeling?"

"Bed rest sounds great, doesn't it? After five minutes, it gets boring, unless I'm knitting or reading. I like to be busy." She forced a smile. Last thing he needed was to hear her complain, especially when he didn't want her to stay in Shallow Stream. If she hadn't fallen ill—well, she wouldn't think about that now. "I'm not a television watcher. I need to stay busier. Somehow." That was a challenge while she spent time tucked under the covers. "I keep telling myself it's only a short time."

"You'll be busy again soon. My sister Jill will come over tomorrow to help out my aunt. She'll bring her two daughters. Those girls define being on the move. You'll like Jill," he said. "Guaranteed."

Kendra smiled. "I can't wait to meet them. In fact, I hope I can see all of the McFarland family before I leave." Which would be as soon as she could safely drive her SUV. She leaned back on the pillows, her head falling into the softness. A lavender scent made her breathe in deeper. No way, it couldn't be what she thought. "Did you scent the pillows for me?"

He lifted both hands in surrender. "Guilty as charged. I bought the lavender spray for my aunt to help her sleep. She claims it never worked. Please take it."

"That's not a good idea for me to borrow something of hers." From Mrs. McFarland's perspective, she'd already stolen her son. "She might want the scented spray again. You'd have to explain..." She let him figure out the rest.

He placed his hands behind his back. "I shouldn't have asked you to leave at our Dimorio's lunch. Leave when you want to. When you feel healthy and ready."

Was that what he wanted? She saw the determination on his face when he had made the initial request. "I know you worried about your aunt when you asked for me to go." What did the rest of the family want? "Could you do me a favor?" She yearned for complete truth, and she knew exactly where she'd find it in abundance.

"Anything," he said.

"Would you mind handing me my Bible from the duffle bag? It's right on top. It would be the best possible medicine to help me relax."

~~~~~

After he located her well-worn Bible and cleared off their dishes, he sat outside. Two acres surrounded the cottage, so he had crafted a deck to break up the endless field. The fringed hammock, complete with an attached pillow, didn't take too long to clean, although the smudge of barbeque sauce from their last McFarland family gathering required elbow grease. If anyone wanted to check up on him and Kendra, let them drive by and spot him swinging in the hammock all night. Before he settled in for the evening, he looked in on her two more times. The last time he checked, her Bible rested across her stomach, like the positive words within protected both her and the unborn babies.

Once the hammock edges dried, he dove in. The June breeze wafted over him. Nearby, an owl hooted. He could get used to this. At midnight, he opened his eyes. The stars twinkled overhead, a promise of hope and good things to come.

"Hey lazybones," a familiar voice called and jolted him awake what must have been five minutes later.

How could it be morning?

"Have you ever heard of letting sleeping dogs lie?" he asked Jill.

"You're not a dog, Uncle P," one of his nieces said.

"You said you'd talk to them about not calling me P," he said.

His sister shrugged. "I did. They must have forgotten. I shouldn't have laughed so hard the first time they said it. You know how kids are. They have memories like elephants."

By the smile threatening to burst open on his sister's face, he knew that prankster hadn't said a word to her daughters. The three of them gathered around the hammock. The scent of baby shampoo and giggles surrounded him.

"I'm up. Stand back." Before one of them, especially Jill, could dump him out of the hammock so that he'd face-plant onto the grass below. He'd been on the receiving end of that joke too many times.

"Why not sleep inside the cottage?" his sister teased. "Or in your apartment? Or even in the main house? You have choices of three places, and yet you sleep in the hammock where wild creatures roam at night."

"The mosquitos and one owl were the only wild creatures. The can of bug spray I doused myself with kept the mosquitos away. I liked the owl's hoots. You should sleep outside sometime. See the stars in the night." His bones cracked like an old man's and not someone who ran five miles per day. He'd pay for the evening under the stars. His aunt must have kept some pain reliever stashed in her medicine cabinet for adults who spent the nights swaying in hammocks.

"Someday," Jill mused wistfully, glancing down at her two daughters.

"Uncle P, what are we going to do today?" Jocelyn asked. The five-year-old, the eldest of the duo, looked up at him with her light blue eyes the color of a robin's egg. She pushed a strand of the signature McFarland dark hair off her still-rounded cheek.

He put his finger to his lips. "Shhh, a friend of mine is asleep in the cottage."

"Why?" three-year-old Ava whispered back. "Time to get up. Cock-a-doodle-doo, that's what the rooster says."

He put a finger to his lips. "No rooster crowing this morning. She needs extra rest. She's been..." What? He didn't want to label her pregnancy as an illness. Kendra would argue that statement and rightfully so. "We have to be quiet. Let her sleep. Doctor's orders."

They nodded, reacting to "doctor," he guessed, and headed toward the main house. Jocelyn kept one hand on her lips. The other rested on her hip. Ava mimicked her sister's posture.

"Hips and lips," Jill said. "She did this all last year in kindergarten with her class. Teachers keep students quiet in the school hallways using this approach. " She glanced toward the cottage. "Who's your friend?"

"Aunt Meryl didn't tell you?"

"I started toward the house then I saw what I thought was an intruder snoozing in the hammock," she said.

"You planned to do what, unleash your pint-sized kids on me?"

She laughed. "No intruder would stand a chance against them."

"True." A mini version of the welcoming committee Kendra expected had now arrived. Would it be enough to bring back the glimmer in her eyes that had faded at Dimorio's because of him? Yes, he'd done that. He couldn't erase his actions.

"When she wakes up, I'll let her introduce herself."

Kendra could handle any family introductions the way she wanted.

"Oh, a woman," Jill said, with a knowing smile.

"Ah, it's nothing like that." Or was it? At least a little, and maybe a lot? His shoulders slumped. What kind of man had feelings for a recent widow, especially a widow related to him by marriage and one his aunt despised? "Let's divide and conquer. You check on Aunt Meryl. I'll see how Kendra fares. How's Robert doing?"

"Great, enjoying some time to see his old friends and get in some hockey playing. Seems like everyone has left for a vacation of some sort, Mom and Dad too. " Jill hesitated. "Are you sure you don't want to switch roles here and you can check on Aunt Meryl?" Hope filled her words.

"She'll be excited to see you and the girls." He didn't add that his aunt probably had enough of him.

Turning, she hurried after her daughters, who had already knocked on the farmhouse's front door. "Tell her we look forward to meeting her."

"I will. That'll make her very happy." More than Jill could ever know.

~~~~~

At the sound of voices from outside the bedroom window, Kendra again sat up in the cottage's bed. The bedframe squeaked. Stretching, she peeked out the bowed window that let in slivers of the morning light. Earlier, she had taken the opportunity to shower, which the doctor said she could do.

"Hey, you're up, and dressed even," Pierce said, looking in the half-open door.

"I am, then I went back to rest. You look tired. It doesn't look like you slept out on the couch?" When she awoke earlier, she noticed the empty living room couch where she thought Pierce might have slept. The maroon pillows that decorated the couch hadn't been moved. The matching maroon and green-striped blankets stayed folded with neat corners, exactly as they had looked yesterday. She hadn't heard him rustle about in the second bedroom either.

"I slept under the stars. When you feel better, you should try it."

As she sat in bed, she braided her hair, still damp and fragrant from the shower. "I'll keep that in mind. Was that your sister and her children I heard outside? I'm sure that wasn't you cock-a-doodle-doing. Whoever it was, sounded quite rooster-ish."

He smiled. "Can't take the rooster sound-effects' credit. My youngest niece has the rooster-call gift. Sorry they woke you. I learned about hips and lips today. It's in my new vocabulary and a way to quiet them, if needed. I'll have to try it on those loud high school students as they rumble through the school hallways."

Sitting up straighter, she shifted her legs and let her feet dangle for a moment over the side of the bed. "I don't need quiet. I love children's giggles, whispers, and questions. Even the crying doesn't bother me, never has. Could I walk to the house and say hello?"

"How 'bout I make you some breakfast? After you've eaten, I'll bring them down for you to meet. Right now, my nieces are having 'grandma time.' It probably won't last too long."

"Sounds good. Do they know…?"

"Nothing, not even who you are, except that you represent the female gender. I figured you'd want to tell them."

She took a deep breath, letting out the air slowly. "Thank you. You figured right." How did Pierce know to do what she needed ever since she arrived at the cottage, especially after what had happened within her marriage? Her late husband said and did the exact opposite of whatever she required.

"I also think you should continue to follow doctor's orders and rest," he said. "Your color looks better today."

Leaning back into the bed, she snuggled under the covers. "Must be all the good care I'm getting from Dr. Pierce. As boring as it is lounging in bed all day, I'll do whatever it takes to keep these babies safe." Even if that meant moving into the farmhouse under his aunt's scrutiny, she'd do it.

"Again, feel free to remain here in the cottage as long as you like. I'm guessing the cottage location seems less stressful than the farmhouse. Here, you don't need to worry about my aunt's questions." Pierce sat in the chair next to the bed, pulling it close as the chair thudded across the hardwood floor. "Want to talk? The doctor said you may have never mourned David. Do you think that's true? If you discuss it, that might help. I'm a good listener."

Her heart beat faster. As she squirmed in the bed, the sheets caught under her legs. "I don't want to dump my problems on you." How would Pierce react to hearing more of the truth about David? "You've been welcoming since the unplanned hospital visit. Thank you."

She skipped the part about him asking her to leave. If she didn't have to dwell on how he stole the air from her lungs, she wouldn't.

"It's nothing a friend wouldn't do," he said.

Was that what she was to him, a friend? She forced herself not to gaze at him too long. Not to feel the strength within his hands. Like a friend…Or was he something more? Someone new in her life ranked as the last thing she needed now, maybe ever. Besides, his aunt would call in the National Guard before she let that occur.

"I told you how David and I met."

He steepled his fingers but remained quiet.

"He stepped out of a fairy tale, how he left little gifts and letters for me on my car windshield and how he said the right things…at least at first. Our lives merged well. I look back, based on all I've heard about him, to see if I did or said something that made him feel like he had to propose. If he hated the idea of being married so much, then why would he ask me to marry him?"

With more time on her hands, she replayed every date with David.

She must have done something wrong. Her memories became similar to a Technicolor movie she couldn't turn off.

"Because you were someone special to him. He wanted to change, is my guess. He believed with you that he could accomplish that goal."

She closed her eyes, not able to watch his reaction, at least not at first. This was Pierce's cousin. David couldn't defend himself. She tiptoed at the edge of quicksand that would swallow her and the McFarland family if she didn't watch her words.

Her throat ached at the words she steadied herself to speak. "After we married, he said terrible things to me and found any reason to put me down. My late husband called me worthless, stupid, fat, and ugly. He said I repulsed him, and I couldn't even make a sandwich, set the table, or make the bed better than a toddler. Those insults ranked as the kinder ones." Clutching the comforter, she shivered. He didn't need to know the swear words flung at her that kept her awake at night.

Pierce stood up and closed the bedroom door. She kept her voice low. Should she even continue? To tell the truth about her late husband's treatment of her and the lasting impact it left could hurt as much as David had injured her. Opening her eyes, she peered at him.

He sat on the side of the bed and nodded. "Even in high school, David often didn't act kind to some of the other students, if he figured he'd get away with acting rude." When he leaned forward like he cared about every word she said, she squeezed his hand harder. Would this help? Yes, she would tell the truth, but she'd risk Mrs. McFarland might hate her even more.

"Names, he...he called me names, cruel names." She forced herself not to look away. Her cheeks burned like she heated with fever. The pillow behind her head lost its softness. "After a while, I began to believe everything. He was my husband. He was supposed to care about me and love me. If my own husband thought these things about me, they must've been true. The words seeped inside me." The names rushed through the air and stung her like sleet that chilled the then-winter air.

He cleared his throat. "Let me apologize on his behalf for all cruel words he said to you. I know it's not the same as him saying this. Did you talk when he left for London?"

Pierce gazed at her like she was a precious jewel, one that needed to be handled with care. Could Kendra even disclose the whole truth, and did she even deserve such care? Tell him about her late husband's reaction to her pregnancy news? That would go too far.

"That's the strange thing--"

The soft knock on the bedroom door stopped her mid-sentence.

"That must be Jill and her girls," he said. "Want me to send them away so we can continue this conversation?"

"No." Finishing the conversation ranked as welcome as staying on bedrest the duration of the pregnancy. "I'd like help to get to the living room couch, though. They'll think I'm lazy as I loll in bed so late in the morning."

"It's tough. I can't say I know how you feel, but it's also only one more day. Jill won't think anything bad, I promise. She's not like that. Besides, she's a mom. She'll understand."

"Okay, please open the door. I can't wait to meet them." Especially she couldn't wait to meet a family member who wouldn't judge her. That would be refreshing. Pushing the pillows behind her back, Kendra sat up straight.

The woman who flung open the door hurried across the small bedroom, her dark hair tumbling over her shoulders in a whoosh. Friend. The word popped into Kendra's head. "I'm Jill, Pierce's younger sister by eleven months. Irish twins, I believe they label babies born so close together. Our mom called it exhaustion."

Kendra smiled.

Jill greeted her with an outstretched hand and a smile as though two old pals reunited. Then Jill introduced her children.

"Hi, so good to meet all of you. I'm Kendra, Kendra McFarland. I was David's wife."

"Yay!" Jill jumped up and down. Her children joined her with skips and fist bumps. Kendra laughed. Whatever she hoped for as a greeting, this beat everything. The children's squeals rivaled the most beautiful music.

"They don't even know what they're celebrating. But I do. Welcome to the family," Jill said.

The words she wanted to hear couldn't have sounded better. Still, Kendra waited for the questions she was sure would rapid-fire next, the questions Mrs. McFarland asked her. No, she didn't pack her marriage certificate, she almost said, to keep that query from being posed.

"Can I hug you and officially welcome you to the family?" Jill asked, her voice soft as the summer breeze.

"Please, I'd love that. I'd like it even better if I could get out of this bed. By Dr. Pierce's orders, I need to stay here as much as possible one more full day."

Jill leaned past the oak night table. "Congratulations on your pregnancy too," she whispered. "Does anyone else know?"

Kendra's mouth fell open. She knew who "anyone else" was.

"Only Pierce. Did…did he tell you?" Kendra pushed away the covers that seemed to strangle her. She couldn't help but frown, and her heart plummeted. She trusted him. He couldn't have told his sister about the pregnancy. Pierce wouldn't have made that mistake.

"No, my brother didn't tell me. A secret shared with Pierce equals something locked in Fort Knox. I could tell." Jill tilted her head. "Something in your eyes gives it away. Please don't be upset that I figured it out and asked you." Jill's voice remained quiet.

"That's fine," Kendra said. "He didn't want your Aunt Meryl to know...yet." She shivered saying Mrs. McFarland's first name and hoped Jill didn't notice. "A little information at a time he guessed would be best." Kendra didn't mention the twins. That news would come out whenever Mrs. McFarland learned about the pregnancy. More and more, Kendra understood Pierce's reluctance to reveal the truth.

Jill nodded. "I'll keep your secret. You should tell her and anyone else on your terms." She grasped both of Kendra's hands and leaned in close. "I'm so happy for you."

"What's the big secret?" Jocelyn, the eldest sister, asked. She leaned on the ottoman at the end of the bed.

"Kendra came for a visit. We're happy she's come to see us," Jill said.

"Who's she?" Ava, the younger sister asked. "Who's David?"

Kendra realized the two girls had never met David.

"Kendra is a friend we care very much about," Jill said. She gave Kendra's hand a squeeze. "Thank you for telling me."

"You guessed it." Kendra laughed.

"Oh, well, as long as I'm guessing, I'm betting you'll buy a lot of blue outfits in the near future." She said the words softly so that her daughters couldn't hear. "I have a fifty percent chance of being correct, right?"

Kendra didn't respond. She didn't care if the babies were boys, girls, or one of each. She hoped for the healthy children God provided. In her dreams about the baby, before she knew they'd be twins, she always pictured a boy with her curls and light brown hair.

Kendra turned to Pierce. "We can finish our conversation we're having sometime later? I want to hear more about what you think."

"Sure," he said and squeezed her hand. "I hope you're not going anywhere for a while."

Well, that changed things. "No, not for a little while at least. Is it okay if I stay in this cottage longer?" The restaurant scene haunted her.

"As long as you want. I'll keep a certain you-know-who as far away as I can," he said.

"Who is you-know-who?" Jocelyn asked. She whirled to face her uncle. "You're not talking about us, are you? There's a mean girl in my class who does that. I don't like it. She's a big bully." The child's eyes narrowed, and her cheeks flushed.

"No, sweetie, we're not talking about you. I wouldn't do that to you or anyone else." Kendra's heart sank at the idea of anyone treating this sweet child so cruelly. Jill wiped her eyes. "I'm so happy you're here visiting me. Do you girls like to draw?"

"Yes," the two girls responded at once.

"See that red tote bag over there, leaning against the closet door? The bag contains brand-new colored pencils, some fat crayons Ava may prefer, and a whole slew of coloring and drawing notebooks. I love to draw."

"I'll get it," Pierce offered. "Then I need to run some errands. I'll be gone for a while. I know you'll be all right here, surrounded by these lovely ladies."

"Wow! These are brand new," Jocelyn said. She did a cheerleading leap, then turned. The child clutched the colored pencils to her chest. "Are they really for us?"

"If you want them, sure," Kendra said. She had hoped she'd have a little niece or nephew who liked to draw. Her other small gifts were still in the trunk of her SUV, too large to fit in her tote. The stuffed animals she won the girls remained lined up like zoo creatures waiting to be sprung from the back seat of Pierce's Jeep.

"Hop up onto the bed, and we can draw together. Jill? Join us?"

"No thanks. I can't even draw stick people." She sighed. "They look like caveman squiggles. I'll start your lunch for later, though. Girls, behave. I'll be right in the kitchen, which is steps from this bedroom. You need anything, you ask me, not Aunt Kendra. Understand? She needs to stay in bed and rest."

"Aunt Kendra?" Jocelyn asked.

Ava clapped her hands.

"Yes, *Aunt* Kendra. Now both of you welcome her to the family."

"We will," the girls called. As soon as her mom's back was turned, Jocelyn whispered something to Ava. "Go tell Mom," Jocelyn asked. "See if she likes the idea."

Ava scooted off the bed, her pink gym-shoed feet with pink polka-dotted laces taking a while to reach the floor.

"She'll be right back," Jocelyn said. "I want to draw something for you. Do you like rabbits?" She bounced on the bed for a second, then must have remembered that Kendra couldn't move around.

"I love rabbits. I owned a lionhead bunny when I was your age," Kendra said. They chatted about bunnies.

"Did it roar like a lion? Roaaaar," Ava said, as she returned to the bedroom. She made her small hands look like claws and added a fierce scowl.

"No, silly," Jocelyn said. "The rabbit has a mane like a lion. Right, Aunt Kendra? My friend at school has one."

Being called Aunt Kendra caused her to take a deep breath. A family, she could be a part of this family. Tears shimmered in her eyes. She blinked hard. Although Jill would label it pregnancy hormones, she didn't want to worry these delightful children.

"We called our bunny Luigi. What can I draw for you?" Kendra asked.

"A puppy? I'd really like to have a puppy, a real puppy. And Luigi would be a great puppy name, don't you think? Mom says we'll get one, but not until Ava gets older. She's worried that the baby might pull the puppy's tail."

"I would never pull a puppy's tail. That's mean," Ava said. "I'm nice. And I'm not a baby. I'm the big three." She held up three fingers.

"Yes, I can see that," Kendra said.

The babies, soon Kendra would cuddle her own babies. Until then, she couldn't imagine anything much better than being surrounded by these two adorable children.

Chapter Ten

Pierce stood at the counter of the yarn store smack in the middle of town and hoped he didn't run into any of his students. Not that being in a knitting store embarrassed him, but how clueless he felt did.

"I know nothing about knitting. She's the knitter, but she doesn't have any needles or yarn. I could use some help buying what she needs." He glanced at his watch. Nearly two hours had passed with him examining every ball of yarn in the store. Who knew yarn came in so many different textures? Finally, he gave up and slumped, defeated as a wounded warrior, to the sales register and asked for help.

The woman at the sales desk in "Knit Now, Pearl Later," looked at him like he had three heads and spoke some obscure language.

"Do you want bulky yarn or regular yarn? What size needles does she normally use? Does she like knitting socks, blankets, or hats? I need some information to get you what she wants." The sales clerk tapped her pencil eraser on the countertop as though that would help coax some answers.

He threw his hands up in the air. He didn't know Kendra. That was what he should've said. This whole adventure into an unknown world of yarn seemed as strange as if he strode into a foreign world. Someone tapped his shoulder.

"Hi, I'm Meg. Remember me?" said a voice behind him. "Is this for Kendra, the woman I met at the craft show?"

"Yes." Help had arrived in the form of a smiling fellow knitter who knew her yarn and understood knitting needles beyond the clacking sound they made. She had to be able to suggest something Kendra might like.

"Let me show you the pattern she admired," Meg said.

She pulled it from a manila envelope stashed inside her oversized bag. He guessed she stuffed balls of yarn and needles inside the tote too.

"I'll go get the proper needles and yarn. What's her favorite color?"

No clue, but maybe he did know if he considered this question.

"I've seen her wear a sky-blue blouse and a purple and pink pastel T-shirt. Does that help? She likes brightness." He recalled her sandals that edged toward neon that could light up the sidewalk at night.

"Spring colors, you can return the yarn if it's not to her liking," the saleswoman said, suddenly all smiles at the thought of a large sale.

"Need any help finding the yarn, Meg?"

"Thank you, I'm good. I know where to find everything inside this store. It'll take me about a half-hour at least to get what you need. Come with me and give me feedback. Please tell Kendra again that the invitation to join the knitting club at the community center still stands. She'd have fun. It's a good way to meet people."

Except that she'd leave as soon as she got off bedrest because of him and his request. "I'll tell her. Thanks for your help. I have a new respect for knitting and the planning a project requires."

"You should knit. You're welcome to attend our club too. It's something couples can enjoy together."

He raised his eyebrows when she said "couples." Is that how he and Kendra appeared?

"Lots of men find it relaxing," she added. "It provides a great sense of accomplishment."

Pierce hadn't thought much about going for a long run since Kendra's arrival. He'd watch a golf match on television and try to keep his eyes pried open if that meant being at Kendra's side a minute longer. "I'll keep that in mind. Thanks for the invite."

A half-hour later, Pierce jumped back into his Jeep, a bag full of knitting supplies flung into the front seat. He took the receipt out of the bag and folded it into his wallet. Kendra didn't need to worry about how much money he spent.

"Hi everyone. Kendra, this will make your bedrest easier," he said a short time later, as he entered the cottage's first bedroom. His two nieces perched on the bed, coloring. He couldn't help but pause and admire the scene of Kendra surrounded by the children.

"You're too kind." Kendra took the bag. "How did you pick my favorite colors? And this is Meg's pattern from the craft show. These needles, how did you know my preferred brand and the right size?"

"Uncle P is a magician," Jocelyn said.

"Uncle...P?" Kendra asked.

He hoped to get his niece's mind off the dreaded nickname. Who started it? Whoever did, it stuck, usually accompanied by giggles. "I'm lucky, that's all. Meg from the craft table at the festival happened to come into the store right when I needed advice. She picked out everything for you. The thanks belong to her."

Kendra gave him an appreciative look, complete with that winning smile of hers that always made his heart dissolve. She held out her hand, which he almost leapt across the bed to accept. Perched on the bed's side seemed a better option. He rubbed his thumb once across her hand's warm skin, not wanting to let go.

When had anyone been so kind to her? She gulped back the happy tears. "No, the thanks belong to you." From the bed, Kendra looked up at him. "You thought of this kind gesture. Did she know about the girls being here keeping me company? Whoa, I see three pairs of big needles and three huge balls of chunky yarn."

"The girls might like to learn to knit after they're done drawing," he said.

"I want the pretty pink yarn to make a scarf," Jocelyn said. "You bought my favorite color. Thanks, Uncle P...Pierce."

"Yippee! I'm going to make a blanket for my dolly," Ava said.

"It'll look beautiful. Your doll will stay cozy and warm." Kendra turned to him. "I can teach them. This was the kindest gift you could've purchased, but please, let me pay for all of this yarn and the needles. I buy knitting supplies all the time. This must have cost a fortune."

He shook his head. "I wanted to help you after you said how bored you feel." She deserved a gift too. Something to make her feel special and know that he also shared that sentiment. It also eased his guilt a notch. He'd be the first to admit the truth, if asked.

"Is Jill going to knit?" Kendra asked.

"No thanks," Jill called from the kitchen. "I have enough hobbies raising two little girls."

Other than running, he didn't. "You could teach me to knit. Meg invited us both to the knitting club." He couldn't believe he actually considered the invitation. He edged off the bed and pulled up a chair from the dining room. "She said it's relaxing and something we could do together."

He clamped his mouth shut. Did he want to learn to knit? Or did he want an excuse to sit close to Kendra and get a whiff of her clean hair? He settled on the side of the bed and decided either or both reasons worked. She wrapped the yarn around the needles and made a row of stitches. Then she dipped the point of the second needle through the stitches placed on the first one. It looked so easy, until he tried it again and again. Finally, he developed a rhythm. The needles clacked within his hands.

~~~~~

"This will be a great scarf." Kendra held up his slightly uneven stitches. "I guess an old dog can learn new tricks."

"Wait a sec. You called me an old dog. I'm offended," he said, hand to his chest.

"It's better than being called Uncle P. I bet you want to replace that old nickname with a better, new one."

"Agreed. That would be about anything. Old dog suits for now.

We're working on forgetting about that other one, right girls?" He shot a glance to his two nieces, who tumbled back onto the bed, laughing.

"Did you like to knit?" she asked.

"Like Meg said, it's relaxing. I should knit in between my student appointments. I could teach them to knit. They'd like it." He held up his practice piece. With the sun streaming in a haphazard way through the stitches, he shoved the knitting out of sight. Immediately, he wanted to unravel the stitches and start over.

"My effort isn't Etsy worthy." Not even close. He frowned at his handiwork. "Once I learn more than 'knit one, pearl two,' I might start a school knitting club." Kendra could give him project tips. Then he remembered that she wouldn't be at his side much longer. Something caught in his chest.

"You're a fast learner. Right, girls? You all did so well," Kendra said.

"Yay, Uncle P," Jocelyn said.

"Ah, Jocelyn Patrice, your middle name also starts with the letter *P*. I should call you Little P, instead of Jocelyn Patrice."

His niece's eyes widened.

"Lunch is done for later. There's enough for all of us and, of course, Aunt Meryl," Jill said, entering the bedroom.

"No," Kendra and Pierce said at the same time.

"We can eat together, but Aunt Meryl acts unpredictably now," he said. He thought of his aunt's admission that she knew she invited Kendra, then didn't have any of the relatives here ready to meet her. Kendra's visit didn't need any more drama. "I don't want to pressure her."

Jill nodded. "We'll eat here, then. Lunch-in-bed. The meal is more like a dinner, so no one has to cook later."

"Yay," Jocelyn said. "That'll be fun."

His nieces huddled together on either side of Kendra. She tucked them under each arm. Giggles filled the bedroom, bringing smiles to the adults. How right Kendra looked, sandwiched between his two nieces.

"Spill on my light gray sheets and my comforter, and I'll put you two girls on laundry duty," he joked. "For now, let's hear those needles clack."

Hours later, his fingers tight from knitting, his project filled with dropped stitches and holes big enough for him to drive his Jeep through, he helped Jill bring in the lasagna rollups. Plates of fragrant garlic bread and piles of grapes took the middle of the bed.

"Think we better skip the green salad this one time," Jill said. "Double portions of vegetables tomorrow when we eat back at the table."

"Aunt Kendra will still be here tomorrow?" Jocelyn asked.

"Hope so," Jill said.

Pierce looked over to Kendra, who bowed her head and folded her hands before she took a bite. Surrounded by the children's laughter and her knitting students, Kendra's color looked better than ever.

Everyone tucked into the food. "Compliments to the chef."

After he helped his sister serve more food, everyone rested, bellies full.

"Ava and I started ballet lessons," Jocelyn said. The two girls demonstrated each ballet position. Next, their leaps and twirls filled the bedroom as their footfalls grazed the hardwood floor.

"Hooray!" Kendra cheered, then applauded the girls' mini recital.

Later, the kitchen timer binged.

"Did all that dancing make you girls hungry again? I made brownies for dessert." Jill leaned against the archway.

"Mommy, come here. Join di-lunch-in-bed," Ava said.

"I'll sit here on the edge. Looks a little crowded," his sister said.

Pierce took his place back on the chair and balanced his plate in his lap. Each time one of his nieces jiggled, his plate full of lasagna also shook.

"Remember, laundry duty if you spill brownie crumbs," he said. He wagged a warning finger at the girls.

"We'll be good," Jocelyn said. "Those are your best lasagna rollups ever, Mommy."

"Why thank you. It's because I made them surrounded by so much love. Everything tastes better when love is sprinkled in. Seriously now, after all that dancing, who's ready for some brownies?"

While Pierce stacked dinner plates, his sister brought out still-warm brownies. "For a certain uncle, I added some milk chocolate chips."

"Hey, thanks."

He had taken the last bite of the gooey dessert when someone knocked on the cottage's front door.

"I'm done eating. I'll get the door," his sister said.

Before she could hurry to the front door, the knock came again, louder this time.

"Coming, coming."

He could only think of one person who'd arrive at the cottage. Someone who remained unfed and, therefore, edged fast toward crabby.

"I couldn't figure out where everyone went," Aunt Meryl said, accompanied by the sound of the door opening.

Pierce could slam the bedroom door closed. Lock it. His aunt would have no way of coming into the cottage. Unless she broke down the front door. He wouldn't put an attempt at that past her. Then his saint of a sister would need to deal with Aunt Meryl's wrath alone.

Kendra bit her lip, and her eyes grew wide.

A moment later, his aunt stood at the threshold of the bedroom. The wind had tossed her curls so that they fell in clumps over her eyes . The long T-shirt she favored in pastel colors stuck to her hips. "Here's everyone. I became worried."

"We're having a di-lunch-in-bed with Aunt Kendra," Jocelyn said.

"Is that right?" His aunt pursed her lips as though something both smelled and tasted sour. "Leave any for me?"

"You wanna come into bed?" Ava asked. "We knitted. Looky." She held up her lopsided doll blanket that honestly looked better than his efforts. "Even Uncle P made one. And I drew pictures with Aunt Kendra. See?"

Pierce held his breath.

Aunt Meryl raised one eyebrow. "Very nice, Ava." Without a glance at the drawing, her voice remained as flat as the cornfields that edged her property.

"It's good to see you up," Pierce said. Her compliment to his niece offered a dash of her former self.

"I spend too much time in bed. No, I don't want to join you now. Pierce, will you take me to see the doctor tomorrow? I have an appointment at 9a.m. I don't trust my driving into town. It's been a while since I've driven. I believe I should start out on a shorter excursion."

"I'll drive you. Of course." After all these months, she would try to tackle her grief. Lessening her sadness could mean her rudeness toward Kendra would also lighten. For both his aunt's wellbeing and Kendra's, he hoped this would happen.

"I'll get you a plate of food," Jill offered.

"Thank you. Double plate it. I will carry my meal into the farmhouse to eat. Alone."

"That's not necessary," Jill said. "Join us. Please."

He'd carry the plate up to the farmhouse himself to keep his aunt from stressing Kendra. None of the others knew what the doctor had prescribed. The less time spent around his aunt, the less strain Kendra would endure. To protect Kendra, he'd announce it if he had to. He caught Jill's eye and sibling telepathy worked.

"I'll bring your plate. You can carry that, and I'll pack up some brownies. While you eat, the girls and I will sit with you," his sister said. "Kendra needs to rest."

"Isn't that all she's been doing?" Aunt Meryl asked.

He wanted to say: "That's what you do," but he stopped himself. He didn't want to be disrespectful of his aunt in front of his nieces, or at all.

"This is different," Jocelyn said. Her trademark McFarland eyes brimmed with the secret.

"How?" his aunt asked.

He caught the look in his niece's eyes like she discovered the best secret ever and couldn't wait to spill. He wanted to leap across the bed and say, "Shhh, please." How did Jocelyn find out? He hadn't said one word to his sister or his niece about Kendra's pregnancy.

"Aunt Kendra is going to have a little baby! I heard Mommy say it," Jocelyn said. "That's why Aunt Kendra feels sleepy."

The dish that his sister had handed his aunt moments ago, loaded high with lasagna and tomato sauce, fell out of Aunt Meryl's arms. It tumbled with a splat, landing facedown at the edge of the bed. The lasagna oozed red sauce like an open wound over his gray sheets.

"Great-Aunt Meryl will be on laundry duty," Jocelyn said in a singsong voice.

"Bring Aunt Meryl to the house. Let her eat at the table." Pierce sprinted from the bedroom. Once in the kitchen, he grabbed a dishrag and two trash bags. When he returned, he started scrubbing and used the second bag to retrieve the noodles and scoop the sauce. Next, he located another bedspread from the front hall closet so that he could remove the stained one. After rushing into the laundry room, he doused the tomato stain that spread wider than his outstretched hand with every laundry stain removal product he owned. The fast movements that might save his bedspread rivaled the exertion his warm-up run required. Breathless, he hurried back into his bedroom. He glanced over at his aunt. Maybe she hadn't heard the truth that his niece disclosed.

Aunt Meryl's face blanched. Jutting her chin, she fisted her hands against her hips like she readied for battle. "I won't take a step out of the cottage until I hear the truth. Young woman, are you pregnant with my son's baby?"

Chapter Eleven

Kendra stared at her late husband's mom. The woman she should call "Mom," but she knew she could never give her that important title, at least not now. Hurt swirled through the woman's eyes. Even more, Mrs. McFarland's breathing quickened loud enough for everyone to hear. She wasn't having a heart attack, was she? Kendra considered reaching out. Holding Mrs. McFarland's trembling hand to calm her. But she remembered the last time she tried that and how it ended. She clasped her hands and hoped Mrs. McFarland would gather her in her arms and congratulate her. Ask if she needed anything. The love for her new grandchild would trump her hurt about learning of her pregnancy from little Jocelyn.

Kendra had wanted to tell her about the pregnancy from the start. Would Meryl McFarland believe this fact? She certainly didn't want for her to find out the truth like this. Kendra's heart ached that Meryl learned the truth from a child overhearing a conversation.

Jill slid onto the bed next to her. "So sorry. I'll speak to Jocelyn about this. How gossip shouldn't be repeated, even when true. She has the hearing of an elephant, which I knew. I was so excited. I should've waited until we were alone to say a word. This is all my fault." Jill squeezed Kendra's hand in a promise that everything would be okay.

"No worries," Kendra said. She watched Mrs. McFarland's expression switch from surprise to anger. Any second and the woman would explode.

"Let me explain," Pierce began.

"No. If she's pregnant, she should tell me. You knew about this before me too?" Tears filled her eyes. "I expect the truth, and I want to hear it from her."

"Yes, she told me when she first arrived. Kendra wanted to tell you right away. I'm the one who said she should wait. Break it to you gently," he said.

"A woman is either pregnant or not pregnant. There's no way to 'break it gently.'" Aunt Meryl sat on the extra chair as though the words weighed too heavily on her to remain upright. "Furthermore, why would she need to break it to me gently?"

Kendra wanted to respond, but she looked toward Pierce, who measured what to reveal next.

"I thought that would be best for you," he said.

Where was the articulate guy whose words rivaled the most practiced defense lawyer?

"You've been through a lot, Aunt Meryl," Jill said. "I think Pierce is trying to say he wanted you to get a chance to know Kendra first. Then once you knew her and, of course, liked her..."

Meryl snorted.

Kendra looked away, and she pulled the covers to her chin like a barrier.

"...then you would welcome the pregnancy news," Jill continued.

Mrs. McFarland stood, and she seemed taller than Kendra remembered. "I've lost my only son before his time. No one bothered to tell me about the marriage or the marriage ceremony, in a courthouse of all things."

"But I wanted —" Kendra began.

"I hope that none of you ever experience such heartache. Nothing in life is worse. Except for feeling left out by your son's supposed wife who doesn't even offer a single photograph from the wedding to share with me. There wasn't even a funeral for my son, or at least not one his own mother was invited to attend." Tears trickled down her cheeks. "I'll leave now to go eat alone. I'm not wanted here."

Kendra wanted to jump out of bed and wrap her arms around Mrs. McFarland. The woman's visible grief made her own heart ache.

"Mrs. McFarland, please stay." Kendra moved toward the edge of the bed. One bare foot touched the hardwood floor. A chill from the air conditioner traveled up her calf. "I tried to find you after your son's death. He had said so little about his family."

"Because apparently, we didn't matter. I only hope your own child never treats you with such cruelty," Mrs. McFarland said.

"No, that's not it," Kendra said calmly. She had to think first and say this right. "It took me time, and I had to proceed with other matters involving his death. Don't leave. This is your home. You must understand that I didn't come here to hurt you. I wanted to meet you and have an extended family for my baby." Thank goodness she didn't slip and say "babies."

Meryl whirled. "Ever since you've arrived, I feel like an intruder." Her shoulders shook as she turned her back on all of them. Then she stomped out of the cottage. The door slammed behind her and caused the wall mirror in the entry hallway to tremble.

"Aunt Meryl," Jill called.

"Let her go," Pierce said. "She's the one who chooses to react negatively to everything. Kendra did nothing wrong."

Kendra wished she could believe that. The pull of her stomach told her otherwise. From the moment she arrived at the McFarland home, she couldn't seem to do anything right.

His sister nodded. "Girls, let's go outside for a walk. Then you can grab some of your toys you brought. You can play at the farmhouse. Quietly. Maybe you could show more of your drawings to Aunt Meryl or your knitting."

"She didn't seem too interested," Jocelyn said. The child's voice shook, and her chin trembled. Turning around, she crawled back into the bed. "I'm sorry, Aunt Kendra, that I told your secret. I didn't know it was a secret. I'm usually a champion secret keeper."

Kendra opened her arms for a hug. Jocelyn dove into them. Her soft sobs shook under her touch. "Sweetie, please don't spend another second worrying about this. No one told you not to repeat it, and you didn't know my having a baby remained a secret. You still rank as a champion secret keeper. Thank you for your kind words. That means so much to me." She stroked her fingers through Jocelyn's silky hair. Remembering how her own mother had comforted her with this action, her heart lurched. "Now let's forget about it and move on. You girls go play, and I'll see you later."

After the front door closed, Kendra looked up at Pierce. "I've caused so many problems within your family for the short time I've been here. I should pack up and go. Right now."

She glanced toward the closet. Could she leave this moment without endangering her two precious babies?

"You know you can't. Remember what the doctor said. You need to rest. That drive home would be the worst possible thing for you."

Kendra stuck the knitting needles and yarn back into the bag. "I came here wanting family. Instead, I created an enemy. As soon as I can, I want to see the doctor again. Once I'm cleared to go, I'll leave. You don't ever have to see me again. Pretend I don't exist."

Pierce took a step backward. Kendra worried he'd stumble.

"I'll let your family return to how everything was before I came," she added.

"Before you arrived, it was lonely for me," he said. "Keep that in mind when you make your decision. I'll let you rest."

"What do you mean it was lonely for you?" she asked. "Everyone in town knows you and looks up to you."

"I don't care about anyone else in town. I care about what you think of me. I want to get to know you better." He squeezed her hand. She wanted to hold onto that warmth. Pull him closer.

Perched on the edge of the bed, he remained near enough she could smell the scent of his woodsy cologne. She breathed in deeply and savored the smell. Leaning in, he whispered, "Even if you can't give my aunt a chance, give me one. That's all I ask."

To her surprise, he kissed her cheek. The bristles on his cheek sent tingles through her body. Kendra wrapped her arms around his neck, treasuring his closeness. He pulled her nearer, and she trembled. It seemed so right, as though they could hold onto one another forever.

"What do you want out of life?" She released her hold on him.

He leaned closer. "I want to live in Shallow Stream. Settle down. Have a family. Do work that matters to me and the students and families within this community." His gaze fell to her stomach.

She pulled up the blanket so that her belly remained covered. These babies were hers, only hers. She'd never share them with any man, not even one as loving as Pierce.

"I don't ever want to get married again." Not after what she'd been through with her late husband. No way. "I plan to be a successful single mom, like my own mom." She remembered those final hateful words from the last time she and David spoke. "And I want to raise my twins surrounded by faith."

Pierce pulled back. "Would you consider living in Shallow Stream? You seem enchanted by our small town. I couldn't live in a big city again. I tried Chicago, and I hated the anonymity. I belong here."

She folded back the blankets. "I don't know enough about this town to answer that question. I have a job and my work colleagues waiting for me back in Milwaukee." Kendra shuddered. Colleagues she laughed with over sandwiches in the break room didn't equal love. Still, she couldn't subject herself and her children to more heartache. With Mrs. McFarland in the equation, that would be a given.

"There's a great library here. You saw it yourself. They have an opening in the same department where you worked in Milwaukee," he said.

She scooted to the right side of his queen-sized bed, far from his reach. Kendra fluffed the pillow, hoping he didn't see the move as an invitation that she wanted more physical contact.

"This relationship of ours moves too fast for me. It reminds me of what happened before. I barely know you." She wished she had said those words to David. "You're a kind man, a devoted uncle and nephew, beloved by your town's residents. But a bigger issue exists." She looked deep into the same eyes that had made her heart flutter. She could not, would not back down from the promise she made herself. "I have my babies to protect. It's a vow I plan to keep. You should check on your aunt. Meanwhile, I plan to leave Shallow Stream as soon as the doctor says that I can." After she looked for the money David had hidden for her.

A few days ago, Pierce wanted her gone. Now it had become her pressing goal. It would be the best move for everyone, herself and her precious twins included. She'd leave as soon as she could.

Chapter Twelve

Pierce trudged up the incline to his aunt's house, and the walk equaled climbing Mount Everest. Each step made his calf muscles strain. His athletic shoes squeaked through the grass. Although his legs and bruised heart yearned for a run, he had to check on his family.

Too fast, he pushed her too hard, and even stated he wanted to get to know her better. With the threat of her leaving, he had no other choice.

"You're here," his aunt said the moment he walked into the living room. Jocelyn and Ava gathered on the couch, and their gowned Barbies headed off for a ball.

"Aunt Meryl wants to make an announcement," his sister said. "She wouldn't reveal it until you arrived."

His aunt collapsed into the loveseat, as though the motion zapped the last of her energy. What would she say now? He could only hope it would have nothing to do with Kendra.

"Go ahead." Her expression made his spine itchy. He wanted to hear what she would state and wished he could put his hands over his ears, all at the same time.

"Girls, go up to the spare bedroom and play. We want to give Aunt Kendra time alone to rest," Jill said.

His aunt snorted.

Pierce bristled. "I'll find her somewhere else to live. I'll check on my tenant. My apartment should have been available already, but the renter hasn't moved out yet." If she even planned to stay that long. After the conversation they had earlier, he scared her so much, he might return to find Kendra with her duffle open, tossing her clothes inside and then zipping the bag closed. Why had he kissed her, even if it was a kiss on her cheek? It wasn't a brother-in-law peck. She had reacted, moving closer to him, welcoming his touch. Had they had a moment more, he would have kissed her lips.

"Pierce, I need some ice water with slices of lemon to continue speaking. My throat feels parched," his aunt said.

He took a deep breath, started to stride toward the kitchen, then he pivoted. "I'm happy to do that. But I know at the last appointment the doctor said you should do things for yourself. If there's a reason you can't walk to the kitchen, I'll get your water. We should listen to your doctor."

His aunt trudged to the kitchen. Each step pounded louder than the last. When she returned with her glass of water, she motioned them toward the living room loveseat and sofas.

"I have some distressing news. I'm sure it will bother you, Pierce. I see the way that you look at that woman. Don't deny it."

"She's not 'that woman.' We've discussed this. Know that I don't look at her any special way." Especially not now, after he had heard Kendra's true feelings of never wanting to get involved with any man, including him. "It has been a tough afternoon. I have a curriculum meeting at school tomorrow I need to prepare my written recommendations. What do you want to tell us?" Whatever she planned to say, by her expression, it couldn't be good.

His aunt gave him a long look. "Your new…friend, I have from a reliable source, arrived here on a mission. She's after our money."

"Aunt Meryl, please." Had his aunt found out about the money David squirreled away? Maybe she located the funds. He could give Kendra her money, and she could leave like she said she now wanted to do.

His aunt took a dramatic breath. "Good thing I found out this morning that she is a gold digger of the worst sort."

His mouth dropped open before he could formulate his response. "Kendra? A gold digger? Don't think so, unless you have some extra balls of yarn and knitting needles around. That's something she might want. But the McFarland treasures, which by the way I didn't know we had, she doesn't plot to steal them."

She glared at him. "Shows how much you know, Mr. Smarty Pants."

Pierce stood up. His aunt hadn't called him that nickname since age nine when he won his school's spelling bee. It ranked a notch better than "Uncle P."

"You have an advanced degree, but I have more than a degree of common sense," Aunt Meryl said. "That conniving girl visited the realtor the moment she arrived in town. She knows the place is for sale."

"It is?" Jill asked.

"That's news to me," he said. "Why?"

"There's too much upkeep and land for me to handle here by myself," his aunt said.

"Pierce has helped you all summer," Jill said.

"Yes, but soon he'll go back to work at his school. I need more help than he can provide me."

A simple solution existed. "Couldn't you hire some local kids? I could recommend high school students who could use some extra cash and would work hard," he said. Cort came to mind.

She waved away his comments as if she wanted to swat an annoying bug. "That does not explain why she stopped at the realtor's office and inquired about my property. She saw the price of the land and farmhouse."

Pierce paced through the living room, and his steps thudded. The overcrowded furniture slowed him like an obstacle course. "What about the cottage? Not for sale. Remember, I bought that from you after Uncle Dave died." At the time, he had hoped it would help her out. Make his aunt believe she didn't need to worry about money.

His aunt pursed her lips, then looked away.

"You didn't put the cottage up for sale, did you?"

"I did not, but I'll never understand why you bought it from under me."

He held back the urge to roll his eyes. "I wanted to live close to you to assist you." He stared at his aunt, surprised she didn't know the answer to that question.

"I'm seeing the doctor tomorrow. You're taking me, right?"

Her voice trembled. Maybe him being here had backfired, and he'd become her crutch instead of her helper.

"That's my point. Being close makes it easier for me to do this sort of thing for you. I figured you wanted that," he said. Not that she appreciated his support, but it was still the right thing to do.

Aunt Meryl stood up so fast that he rushed to her side expecting she'd tumble. "That young woman thinks we're wealthy after she found out the price of my home and land. That's why she wanted to visit us." She jabbed her finger in the air. "Stay away from her. She's trouble with a capital T, followed by an exclamation point."

Trouble? His aunt had to be kidding. He wasn't laughing.

"Kendra wanted to tell us all in person about the marriage and the baby," he said. "She couldn't have known about the property before she arrived."

"I'm guessing it wasn't the fun and exciting announcement she dreamed of," Jill said. Getting up from the love seat, his sister strolled across the room and put a hand on her aunt's shoulder. "Why not get to know her? She's giving birth to your grandchild. She seems really sweet. I have a great feeling about her." His sister headed to the kitchen, and he anticipated what would happen next. Motioning the two of them forward, they both followed Jill. Opening the kitchen pantry, his sister reached for the container of assorted teas. "Let's take a deep breath. I'll make us all tea, which always helps to relax. I'll grab that tin of tea biscuits and..."

His aunt waved away Jill's words. "Yes, Kendra is having a baby. How do we know it's his?"

Returning the box of tea to the cabinet and closing the cabinet door, his sister never reached for his aunt's favorite china teacups and saucers. Instead, she turned to him.

Pierce needed a moment to collect his emotions. His jaw clenched. How dare his aunt make such an unfounded accusation toward Kendra?

"How do we know she spent even a second married to him?" his aunt added.

If he didn't take a deep breath, his words would explode loud enough to rival a lion's roar. "That's enough. Not another negative word said about Kendra."

His aunt had once been considered the town beauty with her dark hair and startling light eyes. Now the anger that churned inside her wiped all that away.

"I can't take any more of this talk. I don't hang around the staff lounge and listen to gossip at my school. I'm not going to tolerate it here. I'll take you to your appointment as promised. Other than that, you have helpers here besides me. I'm taking a break." When Jill looked his way again, he mouthed, *Sorry.*

"I'll take care of things here," his sister said. "Do you also want me to call Joel Martin? I'm happy to do so."

Pierce shook his head. "I know Joel Martin wants you to get back to work at his office as soon as possible. "

She crossed her arms over her chest and her smile disappeared. "I'm not ready yet to work outside the home. Rob and I have an agreement about when that will occur. We won't be rushed."

He nodded. "He'll have to wait a while on his top realtor. Contacting him will only get his hopes up. I'll go talk to him, but I need to think about what I will say first," Pierce said. He tucked the kitchen chair under the table that he had pulled out for his aunt, who still stood.

"Where are you going?" his aunt asked.

He shrugged, glad his nieces played upstairs to keep them from his raised voice. Their muffled giggles filtered down the stairway. "Not here. Not until you can talk about Kendra with the respect and kindness she deserves."

Where would he go? The cottage would be his first choice. He peered toward his second home with ivy that dangled from the windowsill flower boxes. Kendra didn't want to see him either. Not right now. He figured he'd stop by school. Check his mail. Then see what was up about his apartment's tenant moving out.

An hour later, Pierce knocked on the front door of his apartment.

His stomach lurched as the door opened. The renter stood with his arms crossed, not even bothering to look embarrassed at the stench that wafted from the apartment.

"Are you serious?" Pierce asked. "What happened here? You said in our phone call yesterday you were ready to move out. You promised to leave today. "

"Guess I'll need a few more days. My friends threw me a surprise good luck and bon voyage party late last night. The place looked clean before the guys trashed the place."

His renter couldn't be gone too soon. He shook his head as he stepped over the apartment's threshold and into the living room. Everywhere Pierce looked he spotted another mess. Dirty towels tossed onto the floor. Pizza crusts with teeth marks were left on the table. A bowl of what he assumed had once been guacamole but now looked like wet dirt. Muddy footprints traipsed across the kitchen tile. The apartment stank of stale beer, cigarettes, and perspiration. Could this be what Kendra experienced with morning sickness? When he stepped forward, he crunched on corn chips and cringed.

"I can't believe this mess. I need to move back." Then Kendra could have the cottage to herself like she wanted. If she wouldn't consider a serious relationship with him, at least the time she stayed at Shallow Stream would be comfortable.

"I'll clean it up," his tenant said.

"Yeah, you will," Pierce said. His neck ached. He shoved his hands into his khakis' pockets. "Do it today. I need to get back into this apartment as soon as possible. We discussed this. You agreed."

"You don't need to yell," the renter said, sounding more like a three-year-old than his niece Ava ever did.

"I didn't yell. I gave you the facts. Call your friends back over. Have them assist you."

"Think you can stay a while and help?" his tenant asked.

Pierce raised his eyebrows. "I have other important matters to handle. Besides, it's your mess in *my* apartment. It should look like it did when you moved in."

"It did look like that until last night."

Pierce closed the apartment door behind him and hurried down the building's four front steps. By the time he returned to the sidewalk, his breathing had calmed. Whether Kendra wanted to see him or not, he needed to be sure she ate a healthy dinner. Up ahead, he saw Martin Realty. His heart veered in two directions: groceries or information?

The bell jingled as he strode into the real estate office. The scent of lemon deodorizer flooded him. Aunt Meryl had to be wrong about

Kendra's visit to the realtor.

"Pierce, long time, no see. You're here about your aunt's property?" Mr. Martin asked. "Come in and take a seat."

"It isn't only her property. I purchased the cottage and two acres of land surrounding the farmhouse right after my uncle died. That's not up for sale. "

Joel Martin headed across his office and to his desk. Then he powered up his computer. His fingers clacked across the keys. "No worries. It's not part of the listing." Peering over the top of his reading glasses, he studied Pierce before checking his computer a second time. "Whoa, you paid full value for that cottage. Didn't she offer you a family discount?"

"Didn't ask. I wanted her to have extra cash. It seemed like the best solution for the family."

He was single, didn't need the money, and he wanted to help her. At the time, he figured he had made the right decision.

"You acted generous, that's for sure. You want to keep the cottage and the surrounding land? I assume that's your reason for stopping by. All the paperwork is correct."

Traffic outside on Main Street rolled by. Someone honked a car horn.

Pierce coughed. The overused lemon disinfectant caught in his throat, along with something else. If he trusted Kendra, he shouldn't check up on her. "Any interested prospective buyers?" He held his breath. His heart thudded.

"One woman dropped by. She gave the McFarland name, but I didn't recognize her. I'd remember that one. She was quite the looker."

Pierce cringed.

"She asked where the property was located. I gave her driving directions."

"Directions, that's all she wanted." He let go of the breath he held. He'd confront his aunt the moment he returned to her farmhouse. Tell her she'd been wrong about Kendra. Again.

Joel paused. "I didn't say that."

That was what Pierce wanted to hear.

"She was interested in purchasing the place?" Pierce asked.

"Nah, I can spot a lookey-lou from across the office. Too young and not enough money to buy this kind of expensive property."

"She asked for the price?" Pierce ran a hand through his hair. This couldn't be happening.

"Sure did," the realtor said, printing out a listing and handing the paper to him. "Asked for this too."

Pierce glanced at the current price once, then a second time. "I had no idea..."

"Guess she didn't either. I remember her distinctly, not only because she was a pretty woman but also due to her response."

He swallowed hard. What had Kendra said that seemed unusual?

"She said the exact opposite of what people say when they come through my doors to ask about purchasing a property."

"And that was?"

"She said: 'I'm so glad it's worth so much. I'm pleasantly surprised.' Never will I forget that one."

He forced himself to digest the sour words. All the way on the one-block walk to Peterson's Market, Pierce's neck ached. The question nagged at him about Kendra's comment. His aunt couldn't be right about Kendra. How would he describe her to a stranger? A beautiful woman inside and out whose happy demeanor and faith never wavered. His aunt labeled her as a gold digger. He had dismissed the comment outright. That was before he knew the worth of his aunt's home and property.

The market's fruit display near the store's entrance offered an abundance of purple grapes that glistened with juiciness. On the far side of the store, cuts of fresh tilapia caught his eye. He sent a quick text to Jill.

Mind if Kendra and I eat alone in the cottage this evening?

Everything okay? Jill responded. *You're not thinking twice about Aunt Meryl's accusations about Kendra being a gold digger, are you?*

He paused, his thumbs ready to reveal the truth. His sister would be disappointed to hear the facts.

I need to talk to Kendra. Things don't add up. No way would he tell his sister anything else. Kendra didn't deserve speculation.

Jill's answer shot back a moment later. *She's wonderful. That's all you need to know. That most certainly adds up. Don't second-guess. Trust her.*

Trust. Not something he exceled at lately, with Kendra or with God. After he gathered up his purchases and placed them in the Jeep's trunk, he drove home. Toting the purchases across the cottage's driveway, he paused in front of the front door. Kendra might be resting. He knocked on the front door as quietly as he could so as not to disturb her.

"Come in."

Pierce strode the three steps through his house's foyer. He would not think about what his aunt said. He would not think about what Joel Martin said. There had to be a logical explanation. Forcing himself to smile, he opened the bedroom door.

He leaned against the doorframe. "Hey, how's the patient doing? I wanted to check on you before I put these groceries away."

"You saved me with the knitting needles and yarn. If I didn't have them, I think I would've died of boredom. Do you think that's possible?"

"Don't know. According to the high school students I talk to, it's not only possible, it happens. Our World History class earned that killer reputation," he said, this time not taking his usual chair at her bedside. He couldn't be that close and be distracted by her gaze and the lingering scent of her body wash or by that smile of hers that drew him close.

She laughed that trademark sound that filled his heart. He could get used to hearing her laugh.

"I hope all those groceries aren't for me," she said as he hurried to the kitchen, bags in hand. Joel's words haunted him. He couldn't ignore what the realtor had said. How would Kendra react?

In the kitchen, he began sorting through the groceries. "I wanted us to eat dinner together, the two of us," he called. Within a few minutes, he stashed away the items he wouldn't need for their dinner and organized the rest of the groceries across the granite countertop.

Pierce returned to the bedroom. She bent and slipped her feet into pink slippers.

"I can help you to the dining room." If she allowed him.

She wrapped her arms around his neck as he assisted her out of bed. He wanted to pull her close but stopped himself. He caught a whiff of her shampoo as she leaned against him. The scents of coconuts and lilacs mixed together.

"I can make it the rest of the way by myself," she said. "Oh, well maybe you want to stand next to me in case I stumble. Even in the best of times, I'm clumsy. You should see me ice skate, or should I say fall on the ice. I'm a pro at stumbling even off the ice."

He smiled.

"Spending time in bed weakens the muscles," she said. "It happens fast."

He stood closer, but he didn't need to do so. "You seem okay."

After he settled her at the dining room table, he went to work in the adjoining kitchen. He arranged the red grapes, goat cheese, and pita crackers on one plate. When he sliced the lemon, the scent filled the kitchen and reminded him of the lemonade stand he and Kendra had visited together. Had she thought of their morning at the fair since it had occurred?

"Smells like sunshine," she said.

"Hope you like tilapia with lemon and onions."

"I love seafood. Thanks. I can help, or better yet, make the meal myself."

"Next meal, if the doctor says it's okay." Would there be another meal with Kendra? Not if his aunt had her say. Now Aunt Meryl appeared to have a valid reason to dislike Kendra.

"I owe you several meals now, if you've kept track," she said.

"Haven't been." That'd be one of the last things he'd ever do. "Stay in town, here at the cottage, and we can cook some meals together." When she didn't answer, he brought out the cheese and fruit plate.

"Oh, this looks so delicious. Thank you. Don't forget about something for your aunt to eat. She'll be upset if..."

When Kendra frowned, her lips pursed, and he licked his own lips.

"Everything upsets Aunt Meryl now." Thinking she had a stowaway gold digger in her former cottage topped that long list of complaints. "Jill said she'd keep the girls in the farmhouse with my aunt today. I hope Aunt Meryl cooperates. She needs some new faces to brighten her day. Kids can do that." No longer could he.

Kendra nodded. "You do a lot for your family."

Yes, but his mistake had been not establishing better boundaries. "Be back in a minute, after I put the fish in the oven. Want your knitting while you wait?"

"Thanks, but I can..."

"I'll get what you need," he said as he trudged back to the bedroom

~~~~~

When he returned to the dining room, Kendra thanked him again. The familiar feel of the yarn passed across her fingertips. Although he smiled, the crinkles around his eyes that usually appeared were missing.

"Everything all right?" she asked.

With her hand in his, he leaned close. "I need to ask you a question."

She squirmed in the dining room chair, not liking the way he peered at her or the way his voice caught. "What do you mean?" The cross-examination returned.

"My aunt made a serious accusation against you, against your character. I want to be direct and tell you. Give you a chance to explain."

"My character?" She put a hand to her chest. "What did she say?" What could his aunt have possibly accused her of now? The woman hardly knew her and didn't bother to try. Kendra's heart pounded way too fast. "Please tell me."

"I should let my aunt tell you."

She winced and put aside the yarn. "She doesn't talk to me. She despises me too much to listen. In fact, I don't want to see her. I know that sounds rotten, but it's true. Be honest with me. That's what I need more than anything in my life now. With David, I've experienced so much dishonesty."

"What do you mean?"

She took a deep breath, the words so difficult to say. Her held-back tears made her voice tremble. "I don't believe he ever wanted to marry me. He wanted that security before he left that he'd come back to a wife. He married me on a whim." How could David have taken their marriage vows so lightly? Once overseas, he probably realized the truth. He never loved her and didn't want to be held back by a wife.

Pierce squeezed her hand. It seemed right; her hand fit in his.

"What did your aunt say?" she asked. His hand fell away and left her hand empty.

"She thinks you're after the McFarland riches, whatever that may be."

"Excuse me? You mean the money David left me?" Perhaps his aunt discovered the money and didn't know David meant it for her. "I hope I can look for it soon in the farmhouse, at least in David's bedroom."

"That's not the best idea. The land and farmhouse recently went up for sale. Apparently, you stopped at Martin Realty. You inquired about the property."

Out of the corner of her eye, she spotted the large pastel ball of yarn balanced at the edge of the table. With one jiggle of the table, the ball would fall. The yarn would unravel, and the strands would tumble into a mess so difficult to untangle. Most people would give up and not even try to fix the yarn.

She let her hands drop to her lap. Kendra dreaded the confession she'd need to make.

Chapter Thirteen

"Please listen to what I have to say," she said. The back of the dining room chair pushed at her spine. No matter how she sat, she couldn't get comfortable. "Give me a chance to escape from under this microscope your family has subjected me to once again." She put her hand over her mouth, surprised by her direct words that had been building as her anger notched upward. Still, he didn't flinch.

"I'm right here. Tell me whatever you want."

The words should've warmed her heart. She had the chance to clear her name and explain any misconceptions. Instead, a cold draft crawled across her legs and gave her goose bumps. He had supported her, up until now. "Yes, I mean, don't interrupt. Please," she added to soften her statement.

"I won't."

She took a deep breath, all the air in her lungs let out with a whoosh. "Your aunt is right. I did go to the real estate office. I even spoke to the owner, Joel Martin."

Pierce leaned back in his chair and placed his hands behind his head. Between his eyebrows, frown lines erupted on his forehead where, a minute ago, only smooth skin existed. A minute ago, she believed he trusted her. Would what she'd say next fracture that trust?

"When I arrived in Shallow Stream, the GPS didn't work, or maybe by then I became too tired to follow the directions. I stopped at this cute diner, Marjorie's, the one with the red-checked curtains. The baby, sorry babies, needed food. And I needed a rest. I ordered a veggie burger and sweet potato fries. When I paid my bill, I started to ask for driving directions. Then, I saw a bulletin board with a list of houses, all with pictures, for sale. I recognized the address I had entered into my GPS hours earlier."

He crossed his arms over his chest like a barrier to her words. His smile had long disappeared. She didn't expect to see it again any time soon.

"Go on."

She wanted to crawl back into the warmth of the bed. Toss the covers and the comforter over her head like a cocoon. She sounded guilty even to her own ears. It wouldn't get better.

"I asked for directions, but the young girl, probably a high school student with a high ponytail and chewing gum at the cash register, said she had no clue…"

"Everyone knows where everything and everyone is in this town," he interrupted.

"You promised," she said. She raised her index finger.

"I did. Sorry."

Had he already made up his mind that she was guilty? "For some reason, this young woman didn't know where the farmhouse was located." Kendra shrugged. "By this time, the long drive tired me. I wanted to be on time to your aunt's house…"

"This time, I'm interrupting. Because you thought there would be a whole group of McFarlands waiting for you. They'd welcome you. Instead, you only found me."

"Which was a good find," she said with a smile. At least she thought so.

He didn't return her grin. His hand didn't reach out to grasp hers again. Although the ceiling fan whirled overhead, perspiration beaded on her forehead.

"I stopped at Martin Realty to ask for directions. I had remembered passing the place on my way driving to Marjorie's. I knew I could walk there. Plus, I guessed that a realtor would know the way around town."

His eyes flashed. Unlike her, he must not have recalled their stroll through the festival or how he helped as she clambered in and out of his Jeep.

"You could've asked any of the diners at Marjorie's for directions," he said.

His tone wavered toward an accusation. Her stomach flipped, and her palms perspired. She time-traveled back in her mind to the first moments after he met her. "I get that now." She could've turned, said the name McFarland, and a group of diners would've given her great directions. Based on the friendliness of the town, one probably would have told her to follow them to the farmhouse. How could she have known that during her first venture into town? David "escaped" from the town at age eighteen, and his decision colored her beliefs about the village.

"What happened at the real estate office?"

She took a deep breath and hoped she could say everything right. "After he introduced himself, Mr. Martin asked me if I wanted to view the photograph of the farmhouse so I could spot it easily, even after I said that wasn't necessary. Besides, I'd already seen the farmhouse's photo at the diner. Before I could say anything else, he handed me a listing that of course included the farmhouse's photograph as well as the selling price."

"According to Joel Martin, you appreciated the farmhouse's high price. That can't be true." Pleading filled his eyes, but she couldn't lie.

She bit her lip. "I did say that." She could leave it like that. Not utter another word. He wanted the truth, and she told him. "But not for the reasons you think." She stood up fast, too fast. The room tilted. Colored spots blinked before her eyes. Clutching the edge of the table, she positioned herself back on the dining room chair. "Believe me or not, I'm not after this land or the McFarland money." She had ruined her chance to get to know him better. It flashed in his eyes. Not from morning sickness, her stomach would revolt any second. She couldn't possibly eat this meal he prepared.

"That's all you want to tell me," he said. "Please, if there is anything else you can say in your defense, now's the time to speak up."

She shuddered. "My trial here has ended. Your aunt can think whatever she wants. If she chooses to think the worst about me once again, that's her decision. I told you the truth, and I have nothing to hide."

The oven timer binged, and he stood up to get their tilapia. When he returned, he held the tilapia with lemon slices and parsley ringed around the fish. The aroma tickled her nostrils and then made her stomach revolt. As she predicted, she couldn't swallow a single bite when he served it.

Back in his bedroom, the ice cubes in her water glass clinked with each gulp. She patted her stomach. "We'll be okay, the three of us together. Somehow, we'll manage." The words that she practiced with excitement throughout the past months only echoed through the room like a false promise.

The kitchen's faucet turned. Water gurgled. Dishes clattered. Then silence. No "How are you feeling?" No "Bye, see you later." The front door closed like a whisper. Before she knew it, she had fallen asleep, nightmares waking her throughout the evening.

The next morning, she added the sweater she'd worn yesterday to her duffle bag. Even the yarn and needles found a corner. How kind it had been for Pierce to purchase the knitting supplies. The baby's blanket she had started to craft, soft as her childhood rabbit Luigi, rested on top of her other items. Her journal she left on her lap, but she couldn't bear to read her words. Kendra knew they included how she appreciated Pierce's kindness. For once, she belonged. At the top of her items, she positioned the Bible.

She grabbed her phone and tapped the number. The doctor's receptionist answered on the first ring. "Hi, I need a follow-up appointment today, if possible." How to get there? Jill, she'd ask her.

A while later, someone knocked on the front door. Would it be Pierce, Jill, or Mrs. McFarland?

"Door's open," Kendra called.

"We came to see how you're feeling," Jill said. Her long hair coiled on top of her head made her look like the fun and stylish mom Kendra always dreamed she'd be. Her own hair felt heavy on her head as it hung limply and grazed her shoulders.

"Hi, Aunt Kendra!" Jocelyn and Ava sang in unison. Their sweet song touched her heart.

"Hi, girls, I'm so happy to see you and your mom. Jill, I have a favor to ask of you."

"Sure, anything."

"I have a checkup at 2p.m. today. Could you take me to the hospital? I know errands can be difficult with young children in tow. I'd understand if you say no. I could probably grab an Uber or a cab..."

Jill chuckled.

"Mom, what's an Uber?" Jocelyn asked.

"Something we don't have in Shallow Stream. Here, we ask friends for a ride if we need one. Girls, before we go to the park, we need to prepare for our adventure of taking Aunt Kendra to her doctor's checkup. You'll want to pack up your balls of yarn, knitting needles, and the crayons and drawing tablets Aunt Kendra gave you. I'll include healthy snacks in your adventurer's bag. Go to Great-Aunt Meryl's house and collect your things. I'll watch you walk from the window."

"Thanks," Kendra said. The sisters scampered to the front door. Once outside, Jocelyn's long hair streamed in the wind. Ava's curls bounced. They were going on an escapade, and the two girls couldn't be more excited. Kendra had a lot to learn about being a mom as competent as Jill.

"Before I take you to the appointment, we're going to the park and then to eat some lunch. Do you want to join us?"

"That's kind of you, but I think I'll pass."

"Everyone is out of the house. I made some chocolate chip coffee cake, and it's on the kitchen counter in the farmhouse," Jill said.

With time to kill, Kendra knew what she craved even more than chocolate chip coffee cake.

Chapter Fourteen

Kendra stood at the threshold of her late husband's bedroom tucked into the corner of the farmhouse's second floor. Should she enter the room? The question wrenched her heart. David wanted her to have the money he had left, but she could wait until Pierce returned home. He'd find it as promised. In addition, he said he'd listen to her explanation regarding the property. Had he?

She took one step inside David's childhood bedroom. Mrs. McFarland had left the room as a shrine to her son. A dark blue comforter covered the bed, and the emptiness caused a stab of loneliness. Behind the bed, a shelf overflowed with wrestling, football, and even a few track trophies. An oak desk lay bare, with the exception of a single pen. How long had it rested on the desktop unused? Old textbooks from high school filled the bookshelf, but not a single book for pleasure reading appeared. Posters of motorcycles covered the walls as if they had been hung that day rather than more than a decade ago. She took another step forward, and her heel shuffled. The pine scent of cleaner filled her nose and made her eyes water. Had it been Pierce or Mrs. McFarland who made certain no dust gathered in the corners of the hardwood floors?

Another step forward, and she might as well look around the room.

"He meant the money for me," she said aloud. She reassured herself in what teetered between an invasion of privacy or a break-in.

The desk's cubbyhole ranked as a good hiding place. She found a broken pencil that she tossed into the garbage can, then she pulled it back out again and replaced it in the exact position she discovered it. Too easy that the first place she looked she'd locate the envelope with her name scrawled across the front. Her heart pounded harder as she looked over her shoulder. What if Mrs. McFarland spotted her here? Or Pierce? Or Jill returned home early with her daughters asking for a glass of ice water? How would she explain?

Where else?

The motorcycle posters appeared flat against the wall without a centimeter to slide in a cash-stuffed envelope. Underneath the bed remained so free of dust bunnies, she didn't even sneeze. Kendra didn't want to lift the bed to peer under the mattress. She'd rather never locate the money than do anything to possibly hurt her twins.

Hands resting on her hips, she peered around the spacious bedroom. What had she missed that her late husband would've loved the most? Kendra stood on tiptoe to check beneath the trophies lined up like soldiers ready to battle. She considered each award that weighed heavy in her hand. Every trophy gleamed. Never had he disclosed his many athletic titles. Perhaps he thought it would be conceited to do so. She hoped that ranked as the reason, rather than that he didn't want to share anything about himself.

Could she find the envelope in the walk-in closet? Only a few pair of jeans and some old T-shirts hung from the hangers. Her fingertips trailed down one of the few button-down shirts he had left behind. She hoped something in her heart would burst alive again that would spark some of the good memories she had prior to the marriage. The anger that bubbled inside her couldn't possibly be good for her babies.

"Please God, give me the strength to forgive him and move on," she prayed.

While she was in the sparse closet without any places he could have hidden the envelope, footfalls thudded up the stairs. She considered her options. Kendra could hide between the row of jeans.

Instead, she strode to the middle of the room and waited to be discovered.

"What are you doing in here?"

~~~~~

Pierce shook his head and knew the answer to his question. She didn't need to respond. He had promised he'd look, but he hadn't yet fulfilled that agreement with everything that happened. He couldn't blame her for charging ahead with her mission to find the promised funds.

"Looking for the money, my money."

"I'm sorry, I didn't start searching yet after I told you I'd look for you." Pierce paused. "Did you find the envelope?" That would make everything easier. It would also let Kendra leave and never return. That fact made him study his athletic shoes instead of peering into the kindness within her eyes.

"Not yet. Want to help me? I'm okay to be up and around a bit now. I didn't look under the mattress because it weighs too much."

He lifted the mattress and flipped it. Any hiding place the envelope could be stashed, along the edges, tucked into the mattress pad, he checked. With care, he put everything back exactly as it had looked before, even smoothing the bed's comforter.

"Nope, not here. Where else would you like me to look that's too high for you to reach?" He glanced up at the ceiling fan. She pulled the chair over for him. His legs, shaky from his long run, trembled as he ascended onto the chair to reach the fan blades.

"Nothing," he said as his calf muscles tightened on the descent. "Anywhere else?" He owed it to her to find those funds. If he spent the day searching, fine.

"I scoured the room, except looking in the dresser drawers, which seemed..."

"Too invasive?" he finished.

She blushed. "Does everything look back in place? I don't want to upset your aunt or be disrespectful to David's memory."

Peering around the room, he looked back to her. He hoped his answer would dash away the worry and consideration that flitted through her eyes. "Perfect."

"Jill offered me some coffee cake. Want me to go to the kitchen and cut you a piece?"

"Her famous chocolate chip coffee cake I'll pass on this one time. I'll look around here, shuffle through the drawers without messing anything up. Then I need to go shower."

"Good run?"

He smiled before he could stop himself. It had been a brutal run, a midday scorcher. The few days away from his usual workout made his ribs throb. Even his teeth ached. But he did his best thinking when he ran. After showering, he had someplace he needed to go.

"Good run," he said. "I'll search the rest of the bedroom and dresser drawers. Go have some coffee cake while it's still warm and the chocolate stays melted. Save me a piece."

"Thanks."

Pierce sifted through the contents of all the dresser drawers that hadn't been opened, as far as he knew, since David left. After checking underneath each of the drawers, he confirmed his suspicion that wherever his cousin would've hidden the money, it wouldn't be in his bedroom.

Pierce headed toward the shower, his mind on the place where he needed to visit next.

Chapter Fifteen

After he showered and dressed, he grabbed his car keys. He climbed into his Jeep. The engine hummed as he drove toward Shallow Stream's downtown. The breeze floated through the vehicle's open windows and fluttered the pages of his Bible. Once he arrived at his destination, he took a deep breath and gulped the summer air. Clarity, more than anything, he needed clarity. Pierce picked up his Bible and tucked it under his arm like it belonged there once again. He climbed the community church's steps, the church where he used to spend every Sunday morning at 10a.m. sharp. Once inside, he slipped into a back pew. The stained-glass windows let in a trickle of light.

Pastor Thomas strode down the church aisle and paused when he spotted Pierce.

"Good to see you," he said. The pastor stood like he always did, with his hands at his sides, his weight even on both feet as though he represented stability and calmness.

Pierce waited for: "Where've you been all these months?"

Instead, the pastor smiled. "If you need anything, you know where to find me. I'll leave you alone, unless I can do something for you now."

Pierce had so many questions he wanted to ask. How could he ask God to come back into his life? He didn't know where to start. Plus, he needed guidance about Kendra. To ask her to be a part of his life, to give him the chance to get to know her better would force him to break his promise to David. Next time, he'd talk to Pastor Thomas. For now, he clasped his hands and bowed his head. He needed to talk to his Father.

~~~~~

Kendra stood near Jill in front of the cottage's driveway as Pierce's sister adjusted the car seats. "The girls will be thrilled to get out of the house and go somewhere. Why not ask Pierce to take you and listen also to what the doctor says? He's been worried about you, but he doesn't want to interfere."

Kendra stiffened. "I saw him leave." Besides, she hadn't been able to get a good read on how he reacted to her riffling through David's bedroom. Unfortunately, neither of them located the envelope, but it had to be somewhere.

After the doctor gave the go ahead, she'd be on her way back to Milwaukee. Following her last conversation with Pierce questioning her about Martin Realty, even her one McFarland supporter would be better without her nearby, at least for a few days. Being in David's boyhood room and feeling nothing made her Milwaukee mission pull at her. "I can handle this all myself, but thanks." No one could help her with her decision to visit the Milwaukee courthouse and obtain a certified copy of her birth certificate to begin the petition process. After a lawyer processed the required paperwork, she would return to Hester, her maiden name.

His sister raised her eyebrows but said nothing. She and Pierce shared nearly identical-looking eyes. Jill's ebony hair lacked his hair's curl. Her thin shoulders carried an even lankier frame. In the short time that she knew Jill, rarely had Kendra seen her without a wide smile that went well with her quick stride. Even when her two daughters shouted or cried, Jill remained calm.

"I can be an effective and loving single mom," Kendra said so softly no one would hear. If she repeated it enough, she'd start to believe the statement.

Right before she reached the car door, Jill stopped. "I'm sure you're right, but you'll need help. No one acts more supportive than Pierce. He'll be a good friend to you. If you let him."

Was that what Pierce wanted, to be her friend? His kiss, even on the cheek, would be one a boyfriend would give. The delightful memory made her shiver. She had wanted to pull Pierce closer, have his arms wrap around her and hold her.

"You okay?" Jill asked.

Caught. Heat filled her face as she leaned against the car door on her side. "Yes, I'm fine."

"You seemed far, far away, in a happy place at least."

In a place she'd never visit again. "I think the doctor will clear me from bedrest, and I can drive back to Milwaukee." Kendra held the door open for Jocelyn and Ava.

"C'mon girls," Jill said. "Remember, cartwheels belong outside. Even though there may be a lot of open space in the hospital waiting room, we will not practice cartwheels or any other acrobatics."

How did Jill know to give her daughters this warning?

"Public library, last Thursday after family story time, they cartwheeled in the play area and almost clipped one of the librarians. Mortifying. I put a stop to it right away. Today they won't do it because I warned them not to. Besides, I can't have us banned from the library, our favorite place other than church."

Kendra chuckled as she pictured the two girls who cartwheeled through the stacks and surprised library patrons.

"I feel like I'm in Parenting Class 101 when I listen to you," Kendra said.

"Good, because all parents have a lot to learn. Take advice other parents give. Unless they tell you things such as don't name your daughter Penelope," she said with a sigh. "Don't share your unborn baby's name with anyone."

She pulled Jill aside, away from the car and whispered in her ear. "Babies." Kendra smiled, so happy she could tell Jill something her new friend hadn't already figured out on her own.

"What? You're having twins?"

"Yes, I am, and yes, your brother knows."

They returned to the car. Opening up the back seat door, Jill boosted Ava into her spot and clicked the car seats closed.

"I'll keep it in mind about the names." She should start a list. It would get long fast. How would she possibly remember all these parenting suggestions?

Once at the hospital, the receptionist called Kendra in before she even had a chance to recline next to Jill and the girls and breathe in the children's honeyed scent.

"I'm knitting you a scarf, Aunt Kendra." Jocelyn beamed.

"Thank you, sweetheart. When the weather gets cold, I could really use a scarf," Kendra said. Would the blustery Milwaukee winters equal the chill of Shallow Stream? Even if she left and didn't return from Milwaukee, she'd figure out how to hang onto the important title of "aunt." Somehow. Her heart sank at the idea of never seeing Jill and her daughters again. She couldn't swallow thinking of leaving Pierce out of her life.

After waving goodbye to the girls and Jill, she took a deep breath and followed the nurse from the waiting room, down the hallway, and into the examination room.

"The doctor will be by when he can. He's handling an emergency now. Why don't you have a seat, and I'll take your vitals while we're waiting? I see here he ordered another ultrasound, also covered by insurance. Do you have time to stay here a while? I can promise you there will be a wait of at least an hour, maybe more. The doctor is now behind schedule."

She wished she'd thought of bringing her travel Bible. Instead, she pulled out her phone and checked and answered emails from her friend Alyssa. The idea of an hour or more sitting alone made her sigh. Should she have asked Pierce to accompany her? She couldn't, not with him believing his aunt, no questions asked, about Martin Realty. If she had told him the full story, he might've understood. Or he might have continued to look at her like she'd be the last person he'd ever trust. That was what she needed, for him to say he knew he could trust her and not push forward with more questions. Was it too much to ask?

A half hour later, the same nurse returned. "I'm sorry. It will still be a while. Would you like some ice water or a heated blanket while you sit and wait?"

"No thanks. If it will be a while longer still, I do have a favor to ask you. Could you let the woman I came in with know I'll be delayed? Her name is Jill, and she has long, dark hair. You'll find her in the waiting room with her two young daughters," Kendra said.

"I'll make sure she knows. I'm sorry you have to sit here by yourself. Wasn't there a young man with you last time?"

"Yes, that's Pierce, Jill's older brother."

After another check of her vitals, the nurse entered additional numbers into the laptop. "All looks great. The doctor will see you after the ultrasound. It seems like you have a good support system. You'll need that," she added, then left the room.

A support system she might soon give up. Kendra tapped her toe. Why hadn't she brought her knitting to pass the time and help her relax? Just when she reached for her phone again, someone knocked.

"Come in, doctor," she said. That was much quicker than anticipated.

"I'm not the doctor, but I hope you don't slam the door in my face," Pierce said, opening the door.

"I didn't expect you." She reached out to hold his hand, but maybe he didn't notice.

Pierce smiled, but his wariness pulled at her heart. "Jill called me. When the nurse told them about the additional wait, Ava became fussy. She asked Jill for a nap. That's a first."

"Oh...I never realized." She hadn't even considered how the hospital visit might throw Ava off her schedule. Here she envisioned herself as someone who'd be a great mom. Like her marriage to David, would motherhood also bring failures? A waterfall of all the negative words David ever said sluiced over her. The insults drenched her confidence and seeped inside with a chill she couldn't shake.

Kendra crossed her arms over her chest. Pierce helped everyone. She wasn't anyone special. "You don't have to wait here with me." The *bing* from the machines in the hallway ticked away the time.

"You want me to leave? Say so. I will. I respect your wishes. I'm not going to tell you what to do."

"Thank you," she whispered. If he only knew how much that meant to her.

"I'll stay, then."

"I want to explain about our lunch. I felt like you didn't trust me when you wanted to know more details about my chat with Joel Martin. Did he go running to you to tell you this story?"

~~~~~

In the examination room, he sat in the chair closest to her. Time to state the truth.

"No, I sought him out. I believed you, but I wanted to give your side of the story to my aunt." His neck tightened with the statement. He rubbed the place on his neck that knotted with stress.

"You completely believed me? No questions asked?" Her lip quivered.

He had to tell the facts as much as she wouldn't want to hear them. "I believed you. I admit I had questions. Still do. That's my problem, not yours. You don't have to disclose more details." He put his hands up in surrender. "My aunt will have to accept that." But Aunt Meryl wouldn't, he knew. She'd hold onto the gold digger theory like a knot around knitting needles.

"You're right. I won't say anything else. Let everyone think what he or she wants. I gave my answer. And I did nothing wrong."

Maybe she'd reveal the whole story, some day.

While they waited, they chatted about the festival food, the unseasonably hot weather, and Jill's daughters. He didn't utter another word about Joel Martin or Aunt Meryl. The hour passed. He opened his mouth and started to tell her about the visit to church. How the weight on his shoulders lightened the moment he sat in the pew, but the nurse entered the room.

"You need to change into a hospital gown. Then, we'll take you to the ultrasound before the doctor sees you. Do you mind going in a wheelchair? It is our policy. Perhaps your husband here wouldn't mind pushing the wheelchair."

Husband. He never thought that he'd yearn to hear that word. Not after his relationship with Lacey crashed. Kendra changed everything, even the fact that he could return to church and spend time in prayer.

"I'm not her husband, so it wouldn't be appropriate for me to accompany her. Need me, and I'll be in the hallway waiting."

"No worries. I'll go into the bathroom and change into my gown. First though, I have to ask you a quick question that's been nagging at me while I've been sitting here." She glanced toward the nurse. "Is the line in the hallway a yellow brick road?"

The nurse smiled. "We painted it yellow so patients and their visitors don't get lost."

Pierce would only hope that the road would lead her back to his cottage, not a drive to Milwaukee.

~~~~~

A few minutes later, Kendra positioned herself on the ultrasound room's exam table. Near her, machines whirred. The overhead lights reminded her of a spotlight.

"This gel I'm going to put on your stomach will be cold. In a moment, you'll see the babies. Want me to try and see the sexes of the twins? It's early, but sometimes I can tell already," the technician said.

"No," Kendra said. "Whomever God has planned for me, I'll love and cherish."

"I'll stay quiet as I check on a few things. Don't take that as anything being wrong," the technician said.

"The doctor will meet you back in the examination room to talk to you," the technician said, once she finished with the procedure. She handed Kendra a paper towel to remove the goop that chilled her belly. "The nurse assistant should be here in a moment to wheel you back."

"How was it?" Pierce asked after she returned to the examination room. He stood up from his chair and held out his hand to her.

"Fine. I can't believe I 'm blessed to have twins."

.A few minutes later, a man wearing a long gray lab coat arrived.

"Dr. Chou," he said. After shaking her hand, he pulled up a stool next to her. "I apologize for the wait. I've looked over all of your vitals. Everything appears to be in order. The fetuses measure the right size. I see no abnormalities in growth. I understand you fainted, and we asked you to spend forty-eight hours on bed rest."

"Yes, I did faint." Kendra said. "I know I didn't hit my head."

"That's very good. For now, you may participate in all activities that you previously enjoyed prior to the pregnancy. If you faint again, which sometimes happens in pregnancy, we'll address that issue. Any questions?"

"I can travel? Drive to Milwaukee?" she asked.

"Yes, you are cleared for travel. You're not from Shallow Stream?"

"No," she said. "I'm not. There's something I need to handle at home."

The doctor stood up. "If you feel at all lightheaded or dizzy, immediately pull over. Call 9-1-1. Your safety and the babies' must be your priority."

"I will, I promise,"

Pierce sat up straighter in the chair. "I could drive you."

The doctor's eyes lit up, and Kendra sensed the physician's approval of Pierce's plan.

"That would be an even better plan, if possible," the doctor added.

"Thank you, Pierce, you've done so much for me. This is something I need to do on my own." Hope filled his eyes. "I'm picking up a copy of my misplaced birth certificate so that I can begin the process to go back to my maiden name of Hester."

His shoulders slumped.

"Okay whatever you want. Know that I'm here if you change your mind."

Did Pierce refer to her travel plans back to Milwaukee or the fact she'd soon leave behind the McFarland name? What must the doctor think of her return to her maiden name? She placed both hands across her belly. The quicker she could return to being Kendra Hester, the better it would be for everyone.

Chapter Sixteen

"Need help packing your car?" Pierce asked the next morning at the front door of the cottage.

"That's really okay. I can..."

"Two pint-sized chefs cooked you French toast. If you wouldn't mind hanging out for about another half hour," he said.

"That's adorable." Kendra blinked back the tears that coated her eyelashes. "Sorry, pregnancy hormones. You and your sister have been so kind." It was how she thought the man she married would be, too, but he had proved her wrong. She wouldn't make that mistake again. "We'll eat here at the cottage?"

"Yes. Don't feel obligated to say goodbye to my aunt."

She couldn't help but imagine that goodbye, with Meryl adding "good riddance" and possibly getting her kicking leg revved up to go. It wasn't the way she'd been raised, and it didn't represent her Christian values. "I'm going to go inside and write her a thank you note for allowing me to stay here." It would be the answer that would let her portray her gratitude while not forcing either of them into an uncomfortable goodbye.

He smiled. "See you soon. I'm not quite sure how the French toast will taste. I heard Jocelyn shout at Ava about not adding the rest of the bottle of cinnamon. Also, Jocelyn almost added cumin instead of cinnamon and defended herself by stating they both started with the letter C. I believe Jill intervened in time."

"Yum, that should be very sweet and tangy. Don't worry. Whatever they make will be delicious. I'm grateful. Jill, she's a great mom and a good friend."

"My sister is a keeper. I'll be back. I'm going for a run. Do you run?"

"Alyssa and I used to jog by Lake Michigan. I miss it. Now that she's in school, I've gotten out of the habit."

She waited, half expecting him to ask her to accompany him on a jog or walk, but he set off on his own. That sparkle that filled his eyes whenever he looked in her direction now seemed as dim as the farmhouse's dark living room. She should tell him the full story about Martin Realty, but he'd tell his aunt. Mrs. McFarland didn't deserve that truth, not right now. Kendra's blood burned as she recalled how she'd been treated by her from the moment she arrived in town, not even given a chance.

Perched at the cottage's dining room table, the blank stationery she had stashed in her duffle bag and now placed on the table stared back at her. Pen poised, she waited for the right words. Thank you? Thank you for not believing me? Thank you for calling me a gold-digger? Thank you for adding to my stress? What should she call the woman who spewed hate toward her? Definitely, she would not call her Mom or Mom McFarland, and "Meryl" sounded downright disrespectful.

She took a deep breath and began her morning prayer. God would give her the right words. With every word of prayer, the anger loosened.

Forgive. The word overtook her thoughts like David's insults always did, but with a strength that filled her body. *Forgive.*

Dear Mrs. McFarland, she wrote. Better to be formal than rude. *Thank you for letting me stay in your lovely home. It was generous of you. I heard your doctor's appointment went well. I hope you continue to feel better throughout the coming months. My thoughts will be with you. Sincerely, Kendra.* She considered adding, "If you ever need anything...," but the woman would never take her up on any offer to help, even though Kendra meant the words. Mrs. McFarland would run Pierce ragged before she reached out to her.

She assumed adding "McFarland" would enrage the original Mrs. McFarland. Soon enough, she'd be "Hester" again. That would be her first action she'd initiate once she returned to Milwaukee. The reason she had to return home as soon as possible. She couldn't get rid of the McFarland name and all the hurt it carried fast enough.

With a creak, the cottage door swung open. Jill waved from the threshold.

"Breakfast!" Jocelyn said. The child toted a cake container that must have overflowed with French toast. "Are we going to eat in bed again?"

"I set the dining room table for all of us," Kendra said. "That French toast smells scrumptious. I can't wait to taste it. How sweet of you girls to make breakfast."

"It will be very cinnamonishy," Ava said shyly. She held out the plastic bottle of maple syrup for Kendra.

"It'll be delicious. You know how I know that for certain?" Kendra asked. She smiled at the two sweethearts who looked up at her, mini versions of Jill.

Ava shook her head, staring at the ground instead of the French toast that appeared lacquered with multiple layers of brown cinnamon sprinkles.

"How do you know it'll be yummy?" Jocelyn asked.

"Because, like your mom says, you cooked it with love. That's when

116

any food tastes the best. Love exists as the special ingredient, the extra secret ingredient in food and everything else."

The tilapia Pierce shopped for and cooked, she couldn't bring herself to eat. How ungrateful he must have thought her. She let her anger sabotage the meal he had worked hard to create. Did that meal include the extra seasoning of love? She'd never know.

"Let's go inside the dining room," she said, not wanting to ponder the question further.

"Girls, be on your best behavior. I'll be back in a bit," Jill said with a wave.

"I always say a blessing before I eat," Kendra said. She crossed her hands. "Dear Lord, thank You for the chance to meet Jocelyn and Ava. Please bless this food. Amen."

"Amen," Jocelyn echoed.

"Yum," Kendra said, after her first bite. She washed away the extra cinnamon taste with a large gulp of ice water.

"You think it's good?" Jocelyn asked, picking at her own piece of French toast. "It tastes sort of bad. My teeth hurt because of the sweetness."

"I taste loads of love," Kendra said. "Nothing in the world tastes better."

Jocelyn gave her a hug, and Ava joined her sister. Their skin reminded her of softened butter. Soon, she'd cuddle her own children, which made her insides as warm as the heated sweet syrup.

"We're a McFarland sandwich," Jocelyn said.

Kendra held on, relishing the moment. Not for much longer. She blinked back the tears.

After breakfast, Kendra washed and dried the plates. Sunlight streamed into the small kitchen, and the heat warmed her face. The light made the stainless-steel appliances within the kitchen sparkle.

"Bye, Aunt Kendra," the girls said, surrounding her with more hugs and sticky fingers. "Here's your scarf," Jocelyn added. "You think it's too small?"

"I think it's perfect. It'll keep my neck warm in the Milwaukee winters. Brrrr."

"Brrrr," the girls said in unison.

Kendra chuckled. Would Jill let her daughters visit her sometime in Milwaukee? Kendra could hope. "I promise to think of you each time I wear it." And she would. Would she also be able to hold back the tears when she recalled these delightful girls?

Jill returned to the cottage. "Bye." She held her in a bear hug. "Remember, we're here. I hope we'll see you soon after you do whatever you need to do."

"I hope so too," Kendra said.

Pierce didn't approach her but, instead, lifted her bag into the backseat. When everyone left, he closed the car's back door.

"My offer still stands to drive you to Milwaukee. If you're staying overnight, I can book a room in a hotel. You wouldn't have to worry about the drive alone."

"Thanks, but I have some things I have to handle," she said.

"Call me or Jill when you arrive so we know you arrived safely. Actually, I'd like it if you called me."

He didn't demand that she did. Pierce wasn't David. She reminded herself of that fact once again. The two men shared a last name and nothing else.

He gathered her in his arms and held her. The heat from his body melted into hers. She hugged him back. Every molecule urged her to hold on tight and not let the moment end.

"Don't go," he whispered into her hair. His deep voice made her shiver.

"I need to do this." She'd come back. Maybe. Without the name "McFarland," if everything worked out as she planned. She stood back and memorized his expression.

"Promise you'll return?" he asked.

"I think so," she said. "I'm not positive." There, she told him the truth. Now if she didn't return, there'd be no reason to feel guilty. Only her heart would break.

"That sounds like a running track away from 'I promise.'"

"Best I can do." What if she returned and the library in Milwaukee opened early? What if Alyssa needed her? What if her regular physician, Dr. Engel, warned against leaving Milwaukee? All those things could happen. When she gave him the chance to believe her without question, he couldn't do it. Her shoulders ached.

"Safe travels." His hand rested on her neck. "Need anything, call. I'll be there for you."

Yes, he would. She couldn't stop herself from climbing into the car. Turning on the ignition, she drove past him. With a hand that trembled, she waved goodbye.

Chapter Seventeen

After an uneventful drive with too many unscheduled bathroom stops to count, Kendra pulled into her reserved parking space in front of the apartment. En route, she called her downstairs neighbor and landlord, Mrs. Syed. Never had hearing anyone's cheery voice in a phone call brought such a fast smile to Kendra's face. In the background, a dog yipped.

When she arrived at the apartment building parking lot, a steady stream of cars from the street her building overlooked made her frown. Had the traffic in her neighborhood always been this noisy? A cloud of gray exhaust from a city bus caused her to cough.

Her neighbor and friend waited for her on the steps outside their two-flat apartment building. Mrs. Syed fanned herself, making tufts of gray hair twirl away from her face.

"So good you are home. I've had no one to chat with the past few days." Standing up and climbing down the stairs to greet her, Mrs. Syed gave her a hug. Her arms smelled of grass and daffodils. She must have been gardening again. "Air conditioning blasts and cools your apartment to a respectable seventy-two degrees. Glad to see you back. Let's leave what feels like the hairdryer toasting our scalps and go inside."

Kendra smiled. "How about we sit here on the stairs like we always do and chat for a moment? I'm not sure for how long I'll be back...not yet." After her neighbor released her from the welcome-home hug, they both reclined on the cement stairway that poked her spine.

Did she have any reason to return to Shallow Stream? She and Pierce didn't want the same future. She couldn't put herself or her twins in a bad position. It seemed like a waste to spend any more time in Illinois. Besides, Mrs. McFarland ranked as the type of disaster certain to spark nightmares.

"I've missed you. My knitting improved. I'll need to show you."

"I'd like that," Kendra said. Would Pierce teach his students how to knit? Or would he give up the hobby? Would Jocelyn and Ava keep practicing without her around to encourage them?

"How's the baby?"

"Babies, two of them, one for each arm." She told Mrs. Syed about her fainting and hospital visit.

Mrs. Syed tapped her athletic-shoed feet on the concrete stairs as if she danced as they sat. "Who's this Pierce gentleman? Your eyes light up when you say his name."

"Really?" She frowned. "He's a friend who helped me. David's cousin, actually, but very different from the man I married. Stable. Calm. Caring." Left behind, this time by her.

"Hmmm."

"What?"

Her neighbor stood, and Kendra joined her. "Let me help you bring in your bags. Especially because you fainted, I don't want you to get woozy on the stair steps."

"I'm fine—"

"Yes, once you sit down and rest in your air-conditioned apartment, you'll be fine. There will be no more fainting on my watch." She waggled her finger at Kendra then grabbed the duffle.

"No, I don't want to faint either. Pierce and his sister Jill were a big help."

As she started to climb the stairs to the second-floor apartment, Mrs. Syed chuckled.

"What's so funny?"

"You can't even say this gentleman's name without your voice sounding higher, more excited. Your cheeks flushed, dear."

"Oh...I'm hot and tired," Kendra said. "He treated me as a good friend. I don't want anything else from him or any other man. The twins will need me, all of my attention."

Mrs. Syed's paused her ascent. Her glance surveyed the apartment building as if she searched the bricks for the correct words. "Don't you deserve love, too, other than from your children?" Behind her glasses, her eyes looked wide.

Without answering, she followed behind her neighbor. The heat pushed through the soles of her neon-blue sandals that clacked with each step. David had hated her bright footwear that she had purchased on sale, and he accused her of dressing like a toddler. Without warning, David's cruel words filled her thoughts. Shaking, Kendra held open her apartment door for her neighbor, who didn't even reach her shoulder. With her back turned to Mrs. Syed, she hoped her seventy-something neighbor didn't notice her reaction to the memory. Once inside her small apartment, she took a deep breath. Despite the air conditioner running full blast, the place smelled as stale as old bread. Still, her arrival home made her clenched fingers relax.

"Earlier, I fixed us some unsweetened iced tea. It should be chilled and ready to savor." Mrs. Syed settled herself on her favorite chair for her daily visits. "I didn't know if you'd be too tired after your long car ride, so I left the tea here."

"Great, I'll get us both a glass. I picked up some lemons in a fruit market and tea biscuits." During one of her many pit stops, she had strolled into a store adjoining the gas station.

As she sliced the lemons, Kendra half-listened to Mrs. Syed prattle on about all the puppies' new homes. With her every word, she imagined Pierce. What would he think of her apartment? Would her neighbor like him? Of course she would. How could anyone not?

"Did you listen to anything I said?"

"Some. The puppies found good homes. I'm happy. I guess a puppy and a new baby, excuse me, babies, would've been a lot to handle. That was one thing David had been right about."

"Probably the only thing, from what I saw." Her neighbor put her hand to her mouth. "I'm so sorry. Did I say that out loud? My dear, forgive me. I apologize for speaking ill of the dead. On the subject of your late husband, some young man ventured by. Said he was a friend of David, and he planned to move to a new place without storage space. He wanted to know if you wanted to keep the motorcycle, or if he should sell it on your behalf. Josh, his name was Josh."

"Did he leave his number?" The infamous motorcycle existed. How fitting that she'd be the one to have to make a decision about the bike.

"He stated he'd drop by again and bring the bike, tomorrow afternoon about 3p.m. I promised him you'd be home. I didn't know David liked motorcycles."

"Me neither. I don't think I can make this decision alone. Should I contact Pierce?"

"You should call Pierce." Her neighbor smiled, causing two dimples to appear, which made her appear younger. "Your young man should come here and handle this motorcycle issue on his family's behalf. That would be proper."

He wasn't her young man, but she didn't correct her neighbor. "To Milwaukee?"

"Why not? You visited Illinois. It's not a cross-country drive. Certainly much better than the sixteen-and-one-half-hour plane ride ordeal I undertake to visit my homeland yearly. Now, it's his turn. Besides, I'd like to meet this gentleman in person instead of you telling me about him. The motorcycle is important, yes?"

"From what the family said, nothing mattered to David more." Kendra wished David showed her as much love as the motorcycle. No contest there.

"He'd better visit, then. Call him. I'll make one of my famous desserts for the two of you. I have a taste for my own delectable *Gulab jamun*. No one can resist. Cook that eggplant dish you prepare so well. My stomach grumbles in excitement at the thought of it."

"You'll join us for dinner if he says yes?"

"I have dinner plans," her neighbor said. "I'll meet the young gentleman, drop off the sweet, and be on my way."

"But—"

"Call, before it gets too late. I have a feeling his answer will be yes."

Kendra didn't. She couldn't wipe away the hurt look in Pierce's eyes when she said "goodbye." Or the disappointment he showed about her visit to Martin Realty and her questions about the property.

"No time like the present, dear."

"I must go to city hall to pick up my birth certificate, which I need so that my lawyer can get me my maiden name back."

"Pish, you can start that process anytime," Mrs. Syed said with a smile.

"Okay, okay."

When the call to Pierce went to voicemail, Kendra stopped holding her breath.

"I'll text him rather than leave him a message."

Her best friend, Alyssa, would have teased her and called her "chicken." She would've been right. Mrs. Syed said nothing, only nodded. A text would give Pierce time to think about her request to drop everything and drive to Milwaukee.

She typed the text.

> Hi Pierce,
> Thank you for your kindness. You went out of your way to help me during my visit. I can never thank you enough. I arrived here safely. One of David's friends will drop by tomorrow afternoon. He'll bring the motorcycle you spoke of. Any chance you could drive to my apartment to talk to Josh at 3p.m. tomorrow? I know this is short notice. The motorcycle seemed to mean a lot to David and your family. I don't think I'm the one who can make this decision about selling or keeping it. Josh says he can't store the motorcycle any longer.
> Let me know what you decide.

As fast as she typed, "I miss you," she deleted it. How should she sign it? He'd know it came from her. Love, Kendra? Did she love him? Placing her phone on the coffee table, thoughts bombarded her like the Shallow Stream festival's bumper car ride she had viewed.

She ended the text with, "K." And hit Send.

"I need to get home and see if I have all of the ingredients for my dessert for you and your young man." Mrs. Syed stood.

"I don't know if he's coming. I only sent the text a moment ago."

"He'll be here. I look forward to meeting him tomorrow. Till then, dear."

After checking the volume on her phone six times, Kendra headed to her bedroom and tossed her phone into her top dresser drawer. This was worse than being in high school as she waited for a text from a boy. Did she even want Pierce to visit her?

Chapter Eighteen

"Thank goodness Kendra has gone, and life can return to normal around here," Aunt Meryl said.

In the farmhouse, Pierce perched in the living room's loveseat across from his aunt, elbows on his knees, fingers steepled. "We need to talk about how life hasn't been normal for a while."

"What's that supposed to mean?"

Despite the scalding heat, his aunt yanked the afghan to her shoulders as though she wanted to hide. In another moment, he expected to see the blanket cover her head with only her dark curls visible.

"You heard what the doctor said. Not only do you need to take your medication he prescribed, for your own health, you need to get out of this house more."

She used to walk to town daily. Stop and visit her friends on the way. Meet a group of women from church for lunch at Marjorie's. He cringed as mention of the restaurant reminded him of Kendra's visit to Martin Realty.

"I don't want to go anywhere this afternoon. What about you?" his aunt asked.

"I have things to do. I need to check to see if an order of books arrived at school. And I have some other things in town to attend to."

"I'll accompany you," she said, and clapped her hands.

Not this time. She'd gone from asking to expecting to demanding, and he'd been too close to the situation to notice. He only needed to think of Jill's raised eyebrows every time he and Aunt Meryl interacted. His kind sister never said a word, but her face revealed her feelings. "I'll go alone. You need to get out, too, and not only with me. Call a friend. Call…" Did his aunt have any friends left after the way she had treated everyone recently? He recalled the names of the women who sent condolence cards and stuffed her refrigerator with casseroles and enough assorted fruit and cream pies to last for a month. His previously always-polite aunt hadn't sent a thank you note or email, or called any of them, as far as he could tell. One of the women with an easy smile stood out. "I bet Grace would like to visit or go to lunch."

Her forehead puckered. "I haven't talked to Grace since…"

"Exactly. She'd welcome a call. You have to make an effort. She's probably lonely." He decided to take a new approach. "You'd help her by reaching out."

"My phone's dead," she said triumphantly.

Striding across the living room, he grabbed the phone from the side table where he left it charging first thing that morning when he anticipated this conversation. Holding back a smile, he handed his aunt the phone.

"Fully charged now. Call. Please."

She placed the phone in her lap. "Okay, I will. As soon as we're done here."

If she brought up Kendra again and said anything negative, that would end their conversation.

"You have the cottage. As you mentioned several times recently, you own it. I think you will always be nearby."

He swallowed the sigh that fought to escape. "What I have is an apartment near the school. That's where I live. My tenant will leave. I plan to sublease the cottage eventually." It couldn't be soon enough. He reached over and held her hand. "You need to be independent. Live your own life. I'll live mine." Again, even though it meant he'd be alone. He couldn't think of Kendra. For now, as much as it made his neck throb, she'd made her decision.

"You won't help me anymore?" His aunt's eyes shimmered with tears. She held out her hand, which he grasped.

Still holding her hand, he stood up, took one step closer, and put an arm around her shaking shoulders. When he squeezed her hand, her dry skin reminded him of paper. "I'll always help you. You also need to help yourself."

She nodded. "I'll try. It'll be a big change. You've done a lot for me these past months and even before that time. I need to thank you more and tell you how much I appreciate you."

What a surprise. "I'm glad I've helped. Call Grace," he said. "Maybe after you meet her today, you can make plans to go to church together." It might do her good, like visiting church and now praying each morning and night helped him.

His own phone binged. Aunt Meryl jumped.

"Who's calling? It better not be Kendra," she said.

"Why not? I like her company. She's become a friend." The temptation to look at the text pulled at him, but he stared straight ahead. If Kendra hadn't texted him to tell him she arrived okay, that revealed a lot. He didn't want his aunt to witness his disappointment.

"You call her a friend? Stay away from that money-grubbing--"

He raised one hand. "That's enough. I talked to her about the situation with Joel Martin and you selling your house and land."

"What lies did she say now?" Her eyes narrowed into dark slits.

He needed to shut this down right now.

"You act as though she lied to us before, which she did not. I don't know about any half-truths or exaggerations. Do you?" He held her gaze until his aunt looked away. Aunt Meryl bit her lip but didn't answer. To him that response spoke volumes.

"She doesn't seek your money." He didn't want to mention that Kendra still hadn't told him the whole story about her visit to Martin Realty. Despite the fact that the lack of details nagged at him, he'd let Kendra tell him the rest. For now, he had to trust her like she asked.

"That woman equals bad news. From the first second I saw her, I knew I couldn't trust her. She gives off a sneaky vibe," Aunt Meryl said.

Crossing his arms over his chest, he studied his aunt. When had she become so cruel and judgmental? "Don't speak about her that way." His neck throbbed with tension. Rubbing beneath his hairline, he tried to coax out the knots. "She's my friend." And despite that, she had left. Even though he had asked her to stay.

The sound of her athletic shoe tapping the hardwood floor filled the living room. "I hope you use some sense and decide on your own to never see Kendra Hester again."

"As far as I know, her name remains Kendra McFarland. Although I want what's best for you, I can make my own decisions."

Her face dulled. Someday, she'd explain why she percolated with so much anger toward Kendra. His aunt smoothed her shirt, a sign that she had something to say that he wouldn't like. Pierce grabbed hold of the edge of the living room sofa.

"I've always appreciated our relationship. You acted like a second son to me, a son I always felt proud of. I will admit that sometimes my own son's actions disappointed me. I always loved him, no matter what he did." She straightened in her chair. "I will only say this once. That woman…"

"Kendra."

His aunt peered at him, dry-eyed. "I hold her responsible for getting pregnant. You know as well as I that my son didn't ever want children. He made no secret of that fact."

True, but things changed. "Is that fair? That kind of thinking went out in the Middle Ages. Kendra would never be so deceitful." He fisted his hands to keep from shouting. How dare his aunt make such an unfair accusation?

"Can you know that for certain?" When he didn't answer, she spoke for him. "You don't." Her deep breath made her chest heave. "Even more, that woman caused my beloved David's death."

"What?" He jumped from the loveseat. Every drop of blood within his body pulsed. "You accuse Kendra of *killing* David? They weren't even in the same country when he died. A tour bus in London hit him. Contact the tour bus company and accuse them of murder if you seek retribution."

"He called me after he got off the phone with Kendra. I saved the message. I want you to listen."

Never had he yearned so much for a run. He needed to sprint away from his aunt and the toxic person she'd become. "That's personal. I don't want to hear the message or listen to my cousin's last words."

"He called me after he got off the phone with Kendra. I saved the message. I listen to his voice, his last words, several times each day. Before I tuck myself into bed and drift off to sleep, I let his last words speak to me. I want you to listen. It will change everything for you, as it did for me."

No wonder his aunt seemed so depressed. Although everyone grieved differently, her actions couldn't be healthy.

His cousin's voice filled the room. A shiver shoved along his spine. He wanted to run his longest route. Feel the air rush through his shirt. His lungs would fill as if to burst. He couldn't take a single step. If he closed his eyes, he saw David. Pictured him right in the living room with them.

David's distress startled him. "Mom, Mom, pick up. Please. I gotta talk to you right now. I know I don't call, but I need your help. Your advice. Right now. Kendra, it's about her. This girl. This woman I married too soon. Sorry. I haven't told you about her. But I will." His voice broke into sobs. "I've never felt so helpless. The news she gave me minutes ago on the phone...I don't know what to think. What to do. I'm going to go for a walk. Clear my head. Call you later."

Pierce studied his athletic shoes, unable to meet his aunt's eyes. His chest throbbed like it did after a workout. How could she listen to this message each day?

"Aunt Meryl, delete that phone message."

Her eyes gleamed. "Don't you see? This is all I have left. Right after he left me that message, my funny, spirited son died. He was so upset by whatever Kendra said. Distracted, he walked right in front of that bus by accident. If not for her phone call, my son would be alive today. He wasn't happy with her, that's clear. Now that I know she's expecting, I know without a doubt that conniving woman ranks as the worst thing that ever happened to the McFarland family. As far as I'm concerned, she killed him."

He wrapped his shaking Aunt Meryl into a hug. Moments later, his shirt became wet with his aunt's tears. "Let go of this anger. It's so misdirected. Kendra did nothing wrong."

Aunt Meryl pulled away from him.

"She killed my son. Don't let her back in this house."

Her sobs made her shoulders tremble. Logic wouldn't work. Not now. He had no other choice. Pierce left his aunt alone. Without even meaning to, he found himself closing the farmhouse's front door behind himself and arriving back at his cottage. So deep in thought, he didn't remember the walk down the cobblestone path. He didn't recall putting in his key. Turning the lock. The lock clicked. The hinges squeaked. The door yawned open.

Was that how David had felt? Kendra hinted the relationship soured once David left for overseas. His cousin's reactions also concerned him.

Glancing down at his phone, he saw the text.

Come to Milwaukee? Kendra had asked.

He couldn't leave the motorcycle in Milwaukee. Pocketing his phone, he hurried into his bedroom, the same bedroom that Kendra had occupied. Pierce pulled out his duffle bag from the top shelf of his closet and paused. Closing his eyes, he breathed in deeply. The lavender scent he had given to Kendra lingered on the pillow. He pulled out his phone and wrote a text.

Hi Kendra,
Happy to hear you arrived safely. I'll rent a truck to transport the bike
and be in Milwaukee tomorrow afternoon by three. See you then.

While he considered writing more, such as confessing how much he missed everything, from her dimples to the way her nose scrunched when she smiled, Jill entered the cottage foyer. He pressed Send.

His sister knocked on the bedroom door, before letting herself inside.

"Going somewhere?" Jill asked. For once, Jocelyn and Ava didn't follow her like a duo of ducklings.

"Where's your pint-sized fan club?"

"With Rob. He came by to bring them home after his vacation to visit his family and friends in Canada. Aunt Meryl has had her fill of my energetic children. She used to love their visits more than anything. Remember? She'd bake her famous apple strudel. Buy craft projects for them to complete. Now she hates everything. She told Jocelyn this morning that she chomps her cereal too loudly."

"That's what anger allowed to fester will do to someone. It's a wound that won't heal. Let's go into the kitchen. Someone baked great brownies. I thought Kendra would take the remainders with her."

She hadn't. That action spoke volumes.

"Did she arrive okay?"

"She's back in Milwaukee. Someone named Josh contacted her and said he's been storing David's bike. She wants me to come by tomorrow afternoon and pick up the motorcycle."

"You'll bring the bike back here?"

"That's the right thing to do. I can't imagine selling it. It might help Aunt Meryl heal." Something had to. He certainly couldn't say he'd done a good job.

"You look so happy when you're with her. I haven't seen you look like this...well, since forever. You two belong together."

"Tell that to Aunt Meryl. She said Kendra isn't welcome back here again. Not that she welcomed Kendra in the first place." Saying the words aloud made them jab at him even more.

Jill's eyes widened. "Did you misunderstand?"

"Ah, no. She made herself quite clear."

"You don't have to tell her."

"I'm doing this for David. I owe my cousin this much. He wouldn't want that motorcycle sold. That's one thing I know." Maybe the only true thing he knew. Would he give up his family for Kendra, the same woman who pushed him away every time he got close?

"How do you feel about seeing her again?" After he followed her to the kitchen, Jill pulled out the remaining brownies and grabbed two plates. She cut two generous pieces before they took a few steps into the dining room.

He ignored the brownie Jill placed before him. "This ultimatum of Aunt Meryl's makes me look at the bigger picture. I'm not sure Kendra and I share the same dreams. She wants to raise her twins alone. That's what she keeps saying."

His sister gave him a sad smile. "Eat. You need to keep up your strength."

He didn't know how to break it to her that a brownie wouldn't solve anything.

"Kendra has no idea how hard it will be. I'm not saying she can't do it and do it well. She's determined. Even with Rob helping me with the girls, I fall into bed each night, and I'm asleep within minutes," she said, yawning. "Look at me, even thinking about sleep."

"You make it seem easy. You're a great mom." He pictured Kendra's warm smile and her contagious chuckle. Despite the challenges his aunt provided, he never laughed as much as he did when Kendra visited. She had encouraged him to see the world with a renewed Christian perspective.

Jill pushed the plate closer. "What about Aunt Meryl? Think she'll come around? She's moving," his sister reminded him.

"So she claims." Pierce wasn't sure putting the farmhouse up for sale without a sign constituted moving.

"You also deserve love. It isn't right that she can make that decision for you. How will you feel if you give up on Kendra?"

"She also was married to David," he said. Pierce couldn't erase his cousin's chilling phone call from his mind. How could Aunt Meryl listen to the call each day?

"Not happily, if I can read through the lines on what she's said. See if Aunt Meryl has any reason at all not to like Kendra," Jill said.

An accusation of murder, whether it made sense or not, couldn't be wiped away with a simple conversation. His aunt remained convinced her son's death happened because of Kendra. He didn't see how he or anyone else could change that belief that she allowed to become buried in her soul. In fairness to Kendra, he didn't feel it would be right to tell his sister without Kendra knowing the situation first.

"Don't give up on Kendra," she said. "I'll take it personally if you don't at least try the brownie I made."

Jill forgot the fact that Kendra had given up on him.

"If she says 'no,' she'll raise her twins alone no matter what?" Then what? Either way, he'd be alone. To keep Jill happy, he ate half the brownie, but couldn't taste any of the chocolate sweetness.

He strode into his bedroom past the bed Kendra had recently occupied. Touching the middle of the bed, cold lingered where she had once rested. Shaking his head, he opened up his dresser drawers and started packing.

Chapter Nineteen

"Please stay," Kendra said, as she stood in her apartment with her best friend. "Or do you have things you have to do?"

In the living room that could be walked through in six steps, Alyssa hugged her again. "You always think of everyone else first."

"Mrs. McFarland sure wouldn't agree."

"You read me the text. Pierce wants to talk to you. The two of you need to be alone without the shadow of his aunt looming over you," Alyssa added.

Would that happen? Even a friendship with Pierce would mean his aunt would scowl while Kendra's stomach churned. What would happen once the twins arrived? Would his aunt's dislike of her transfer to the twins also? She trembled at the thought of anyone resenting innocent babies.

"Meet him. Say hi," Kendra said. She tried to keep her voice from shaking. Pierce, she'd see him in a few minutes. Once again, their meeting would occur at 3p.m., like when she believed she'd meet the whole McFarland family. Ironic. Alone, they could discuss the future, if one existed.

Alyssa paused. "I thought you were friends. That's what you said. You don't need my opinion of him if you're not. I don't need to be your only friend."

"Pierce and I are friends." Was this even true? Kendra had never lied to her best friend, and she hoped she hadn't told her first untruth. "I can't stop thinking about him. It hasn't been that long since David died. This seems wrong."

Alyssa placed her hand on her shoulder with a reassuring pat like the ER doctor had done, but her friend's action included the warmth Kendra craved.

Taking a step forward, she wrapped herself in her friend's embrace. Alyssa's hair trailed onto Kendra's shoulder.

Leaning back, her friend held her at arms' length. "Oh honey, you're right, it hasn't been that long. I think maybe you and David rushed into marriage. You can't change the past. Love doesn't always occur on our schedules."

Could she love Pierce? "If it is love...and I'm not sure that it is, I don't want to make the same mistake I made with David and charge ahead with our relationship." She shivered. "I didn't know him at all when we married. You saw the results. Never would I have married any man who asked me to do what he did." She shuddered and involuntarily placed a protective hand across her abdomen.

"Let Pierce know what matters to you. Take it one step at a time."

"There's the bell. He must be here," Kendra said. She took a deep breath and tried to smooth her curls. If her whole body reacted to even the thought of Pierce, would she melt into a puddle when she saw him again? When she answered the door, the man there wasn't Pierce. He had skin the color of wet sand and dark brown eyes that twinkled.

"Hi, I'm Josh, David's friend. You must be Kendra."

"Yes, thanks for coming by," she said and peered around his shoulder. Kendra saw the motorcycle in the driveway. The sun's rays bouncing off the fenders made the motorcycle glisten. "Please, come in. Pierce will be here any second. This is my friend, Alyssa."

Josh stopped in the middle of the living room and his mouth opened slightly, like he had something important to say but forgot what. Kendra chuckled as he regained his composure and shook her best friend's hand.

"Nice to meet you, Alyssa. Do you live around here?" he asked.

As they chatted, Alyssa's scalp reddened through her blonde hair.

The doorbell rang again, and Kendra ushered in Mrs. Syed, bringing the promised dessert. "I'll only stay a moment to say hello, dear."

"This is my neighbor, Mrs. Syed, everyone."

"Hi," Josh said, without taking his eyes off Alyssa.

With the third doorbell ring, Kendra's heart raced. This one had to be Pierce. Who else would drop by? She couldn't believe how it felt like days dragged by without him. She rushed to open the front door.

"Hi, Pierce. Great to see you."

"And you," he said. He reached in for a quick hug that left her wanting more. "Are you feeling okay?"

"Never better." As soon as she had left the farm, all her energy had returned. "How is everyone, Jill, those two sweet girls…um…and your aunt?"

"Everyone is doing well," he said.

"This is Mrs. Syed, my landlord. She made us a dessert for later."

The sweet scent of the dessert perfumed the room.

"Hi, Mrs. Syed. I'm Pierce McFarland. It's a pleasure to meet you. And I can't wait to sample that dessert you're holding."

She held out the plate to him. "A man who appreciates good food has an equally good heart." Mrs. Syed beamed.

Pierce placed the dessert onto the dining room table. "Hi, Josh. Let's go outside and take a look at the bike. I looked it over when I arrived, and it appears to be in perfect shape."

Kendra bit her lip. He acted like a neighbor she waved to at the grocery store as she strolled through the produce aisle. Any feelings for her had disappeared along with the accusations his aunt had made.

"I knew how much this bike meant to David.

"I kept that baby garaged and covered. I drove it a little to keep the juices running. Kendra, I'm sorry about your loss. I should've said that sooner." As the two men headed toward the front door, Josh took a glance back at Alyssa. "I was distracted. David will be missed by everyone who knew him."

"Thank you." Hollowness filled her stomach. What kind of person didn't long for her deceased husband after such a short time had passed? Although the anger didn't burn and bubble like it had, her heart no longer cracked. The word pushed through her thoughts again. *Forgive.*

I forgive you, David, for what you asked me to do. More than anything else, that showed we never knew each other. It is probably for the best. I will raise these two precious babies alone.

Pierce and Josh went outside to discuss the motorcycle and make arrangements, as Mrs. Syed hugged her and waved goodbye.

"I don't know what occurred," Alyssa said, after Mrs. Syed closed the apartment's front door. Her eyes widened. "Did you see how I reacted to Josh? That's never happened to me before. Ever."

As she reached over and gave her friend a quick hug, Kendra laughed. "I saw. Love tumbles into your life when you least expect it. Josh reacted to you, too. At least you share mutual feelings." Similar to how she had behaved when she met David. She wouldn't wish what ended up happening to her on anyone.

"What should I do?" She wrung her hands.

Kendra shrugged and tried not to giggle. Alyssa deserved someone kind in her life. Only time would tell if that kindness would come through Josh.

Twenty minutes later, both men returned, but Kendra's eyes couldn't be pulled away from gazing at Pierce.

"We have it all worked out," Pierce said. "I'll bring the motorcycle back to the farm in the moving truck I rented. We've already loaded the bike, and it's ready to go."

"That's great," Kendra said. "Alyssa, Josh, would you like to join us for dinner?" As much as she enjoyed company, a small part of her hoped they both said no. Having time alone with Pierce would be a precious treasure.

"Something smells delicious," Josh said. "I'm in." He looked to Alyssa.

"That's kind of you, but I think you two need some time alone to chat," her friend said. "How about I take two pieces of this delicious-looking dessert on a plate? Josh and I can stop and get some coffee at The Edge and sample this dessert. Would that be okay with everyone?"

"I'd like that," Josh said with a shy smile.

"Josh is a good guy," Pierce said after the other two left and they stood alone for the first time that afternoon.

"Who knows? Maybe the two of them will end up being a great couple." Would she and Pierce also be a loving couple?

"Mind if I sit down?" he asked.

"Sorry, where are my manners? May I get you some ice water? You must be hot after hoisting that motorcycle into the truck."

"Wasn't bad with Josh's help."

She motioned toward the living room. "Let's go sit down and talk."

Before he reclined onto her loveseat, Pierce rested his hand on the top of the living room rocking chair. Did he imagine her someday rocking in the chair as she calmed and cuddled her twins?

As soon as he sat, his face turned serious. "Is that what we are? A couple? Or are we friends? I'd like to move forward and begin dating, if you'd consider that."

Kendra gulped and patted her stomach. "I'm not sure I can. I need to tell you something. It's about my last conversation with your cousin prior to his death." No longer would she refer to him as her late husband.

Kendra perched next to Pierce on the living room loveseat that seemed to have shrunk in size. She tried not to notice his thigh pressed against hers. Behind her, open curtains let bright light spill into the room, providing the airy opposite of the farmhouse's dark living room.

"I want to hear whatever you want to tell me." His expression remained more serious than she'd ever seen him.

She took a deep breath. "I learned the morning he died I was expecting a baby, and I was over the moon. I figured David might feel a little frightened. He'd always asked me how much I spent on groceries each week, so I knew he worried about money." This was so different from the guy who thought a $500 air balloon ride didn't cost too much when they dated. "Still…this baby, now babies, were both of ours. So when I told him…" She put her head in her hands, not sure she could share this with Pierce.

"It's okay," he said. Pierce reached over and put a comforting hand on hers.

The mountain she balanced on her back all these weeks crumbled.

136

The facts crashed down on her like jagged stones that jabbed at her. "He told me...he didn't want a baby. Not now with me, and not ever." Her voice cracked. "I couldn't understand. We talked about children, how many we wanted to have and when. Yes, this pregnancy occurred a year ahead of schedule, but still." She squeezed his hand. Hard. The sun hid behind a cloud, throwing a dark shadow across the room, exactly how her heart felt when she recalled her late husband's words. She had to say the rest. "To my shock, David demanded...I have an abortion." A tear trickled down her cheek before she wiped it away with her palm. "I told him I wouldn't consider that option. It's against my faith, and I wouldn't ever do such a thing. He said there was nothing to discuss. If I went ahead with the pregnancy, he'd file for divorce."

"I'm sorry, Kendra."

Nodding, she forced herself to continue. "His words pulverized me. I don't know if he met someone in London, or while away from me he decided he didn't want to be married." Fatigue tugged at her with the confession. She wanted to close her eyes and melt against his shoulder. She couldn't fall asleep with her sadness saturating her thoughts. "I'll never know. He didn't love me."

"David was impulsive. He may have changed his mind later."

She shook her head. "He said a baby with me ranked as the last thing he ever wanted. He told the truth. Maybe that was the first true thing he ever said to me." She looked down at her shaking hands.

Pierce wrapped her in a gentle hug, the kind Alyssa gave her. He smelled like the outdoors, the freshest spring grass, and if hope had a scent, that too.

When she heaved under his embrace, he held her tighter. Under the strength of his embrace, she let her eyes flutter close. Finally, someone besides Alyssa knew the burden that withered her heart when anyone mentioned David.

He smoothed back her hair and pushed the strands off her forehead. His touch brought the warmth and comfort of a calm wave. Leaning into him, she closed her eyes and let her anger about David's demand float away.

"Thank you for telling me. That must have been very difficult."

She pulled back. "I'm glad you know the whole truth. Oh..."

"What?" He jumped to his feet and leaned over her. "What's wrong?"

"It's nothing." She touched his forearm. "It's not like at Dimorio's. No hospital visits to follow. I'm guessing my nerves made my stomach flutter. But eventually I'll feel my babies moving and full of life."

Placing a hand on her shoulder, he gave it a squeeze. He let his hand linger.

"How could he have wanted..." she began. Tears choked back her unspoken words.

"Don't think about David." He pulled her close, and she let herself relax into his embrace. "These are your babies, loved and cherished already."

~~~~~

While she rested her head against his shoulder, he ran his hand through the length of her curls, the soft strands silkier than they appeared. He comforted her when she needed it most. Nothing more. Then why did he want to let go of her hair and tilt her head up for a kiss? He released her. That was not what Kendra needed from him, not now, and possibly not ever. She never answered his question about the possibility of a relationship. That silence revealed much.

"Is something wrong?" She looked up to him with her soft brown eyes. From the heat of being held close, her cheeks were flushed.

"You don't need to worry about the motorcycle." Why had he brought the conversation back to the motorcycle? He wanted to talk about the possibility of them, not discuss the bike.

"Oh. Thanks," she said, frowning slightly. "Um...Do I owe you any money?"

Seriously? He shook his head as the buzzer for their dinner shrilled. Pierce stepped toward the galley kitchen entryway. The kitchen's white cabinets made the space appear larger. "What can I do to help?"

"Have a seat at the table."

He settled into the dining room chair as the delicious aroma of roasted eggplant filled the eating area. The whole apartment reminded him of a beach resort with blue and white trim. Kendra had even fashioned a centerpiece out of different-sized seashells that circled a vase of fresh-cut daisies. After dinner, he'd have to ask her if she loved the beach. He pictured them walking along the beach together, holding hands, the waves crashing over their feet as they dodged the tide.

"Now it's your turn to relax and chat with me while I get the food on the table," she said with a smile.

"You're a great cook," he said an hour later. Pierce couldn't remember when he enjoyed a dinner more. Picking up the china plates, he headed toward the kitchen. "I relished that meal, and I liked the company even better."

"If you know what's good for you, you'll unhand those dishes. You're a guest, remember? Sound familiar?"

He put his hands up in surrender, then followed her into the kitchen no wider than the farmhouse's front hallway. No surprise that the walls included two paintings that contained inspirational verses.

"You did me and my aunt a big favor by not selling David's bike," he said. "You could've easily never contacted me or the family again." He hoped she knew that would've been the last thing he'd ever want.

Her eyes widened. "Don't tell me you're going to ride the motorcycle once you get it back home."

"Ah, no, I like to be surrounded by car doors. It will make my aunt happy to see her son's bike again."

She rinsed the last dish from their dinner as the soap bubbles danced into the drain. "I'd like to see your aunt happy. Or I'd at least like to hear she's doing better."

Would he have been as generous with forgiveness if the situation were reversed? "Aunt Meryl hasn't been happy in a while. I'm not sure she fully recovered from her husband dying young, either. Her whole life had been the family and the farm. And now..." Aunt Meryl had nothing.

She dried her hands on the blue-checked towels positioned next to the sink. "With God's help, I've asked David to forgive me," she blurted. "I did something wrong. I don't think it's ever one person's fault when a relationship crumbles into small pieces beyond repair. I also told him I needed to forgive him to move on with my life."

"Does that mean..." Pierce tried to quiet his soaring heart. He put his hand on hers. She could be ready for a relationship with him.

Kendra turned back toward the countertop as though the stainless-steel sink she stood in front of glinted with answers. "I need to be here for my twins. They're what matters now. I'm not in any position to start any kind of romantic relationship. Maybe when they're older, in school..."

There'd always be something. Pierce pictured all the pivotal times that would occur in the twins' lives. An excuse popped up with each milestone: preschool, kindergarten, middle school, and high school. He didn't fit in with any of these options. If she loved him, she'd let him be a part of her life now. No hesitation.

In the tiny kitchen as he faced her, he only had to lift his arms around her shoulders to embrace her and pull her close. Feel the beat of her heart pressed against his chest "I get it. Like my aunt, I have some anger too. I want to get rid of that." Lacey hadn't gone out of his life that long ago. Even though he hadn't given her a second thought, he always suggested to students to leave time to grieve. Listening to his own advice would be a smart idea.

She smoothed back her curls and took a step closer to him. If he reached out, his hands could once again run through her amazing hair.

"Maybe we could get to know each other privately. I know I said I wanted family, but perhaps with less family surrounding us…" she said. "You could come visit me again."

Secret, she wanted to keep their relationship hidden. He stayed silent, not sure what to say. Maybe another visit would be hard on the babies once they were born. As they grew older… He didn't want to confuse them. Questions pulled at him like the tide. He pointed to the oceanfront pictures on the wall.

"Are you a beach lover?" *Say yes.*

"I am, but I'm not a fan of crowded summer-only beaches. I'd like to go to Nantucket again in their off season or stroll along Lake Michigan on a day everyone else complains it's too cold and windy."

"Me too." They shared the belief that beaches deserved to be visited and strolled on, even if raindrops transformed the sand into mud, or snowflakes blanketed the beachfront. "We could go together." Was he pushing too hard?

When she didn't answer, Pierce took action. He took her hand and led her back to the living room couch. Her fingers fit together with his like two puzzle pieces snapped together. Once on the couch, he placed a pillow behind her head. At least he could make her comfortable for the news that could mean he'd lose her.

"What's going on?" she asked.

"If there's even a chance we can start a relationship, it needs to begin with honesty. I need to tell you something you're guaranteed not to like."

She bit her lip, and he squeezed her hand. He refused to sugar coat this, no matter how much it would hurt her. Kendra deserved to know the truth about what his aunt believed, even if he knew the ridiculous story outshone the worst tabloid news.

Chapter Twenty

Somehow, Kendra fought back the tears that pushed at the back of her eyes with the force of a waterfall, in reaction to what Pierce had just told her. "Are you sure you heard her right?" She stood up suddenly and caused the quilt her grandma crafted to tumble to the living room floor. Shaking so hard, she couldn't bend over and reclaim the treasured quilt. "I killed her son? Unbelievable. What a wretched thing for her to say. I know she's grieving, but that's crazy. No wonder she hated me the moment she saw me." Something twisted in her stomach. She stomped across the living room and wanted to grab her phone. Meryl McFarland, even in her misery, couldn't get away with spouting lies about her. This had gone too far and had to stop now.

He held out his hand to her as an invitation for her to sit next to him again and snuggle on her loveseat. As much as she wanted to grasp his hand and let the warmth of his touch surge through her, she couldn't. Not this time. Anger surged through every step of hers that thudded through the living room. Wasn't he a McFarland? Why didn't he tell off his aunt in a way that ensured she would never bring up the subject again?

"I can't imagine my aunt ever intended to throw you any welcome-to-the-family party. As much as I don't want to hurt her, I also don't want any problems for you or the twins."

She'd never be accepted. The babies were Mrs. McFarland's grandchildren. She didn't even care about her only grandchildren. Who did that? In her spare bedroom sat a crib and linens, gifts from her library colleagues. Kendra had decorated the nursery with woodland animals encircled by inspirational verses. Would Mrs. McFarland even bother to step foot into the nursery once the babies arrived?

She took deep breaths as though she'd surfaced after having been shoved underwater and held there a moment too long. "I'm stunned. First, she called me a gold digger. Now, I've been promoted to murderess. What's next? Second thought, I don't think she could say anything worse." Kendra paced in front of the love seat where Pierce sat. "What would she say if she knew her son's last words to me?" The blood in her heart boiled. How dare Mrs. McFarland act like her son did nothing wrong? David wanted to divorce her so his mom would never even know Kendra or the babies existed.

"Don't tell my aunt. She won't believe you."

"It's the truth," she said. She pressed her hands together to keep them from shaking.

"I know that. It will only make her dislike you more. She'll add liar to her list of complaints. You've nothing to gain here," he said. "Give her time."

She had given Mrs. McFarland enough time, thank you very much. The woman would not change her opinion of her even if Kendra won a global humanitarian award. Even more, Mrs. McFarland would never let Pierce out of her clutches. Kendra looked into his deep eyes, wanting to memorize every detail on his face, from his high cheekbones to his thick eyebrows. This new revelation changed everything. How could they ever have a relationship when his aunt remained so much a part of his life? And she wasn't about to ask him to alter his life for her. She paused mid-step.

"You…you better leave," Kendra said. "We can't continue our friendship. She'll get what she wants, and she wants me out of all the McFarlands' lives. My name will be back to Hester as soon as I can make the change. As I mentioned, that's why I returned home."

He jammed his hands into his jean pockets. "Can I call or text or email?"

She weighed her options. "Not now. That's not a good idea. Plus, I'll be back to work soon."

"I'm willing to deal with my aunt. I stood up for you, and I always will."

She raised her eyebrows. Could she believe that statement?

"Know I will handle her. I promise I will. Make sure you say what you mean. Don't answer." He put up both hands in surrender. "Not yet. Think about what you want. For now, I'm leaving. Thank you for dinner. I enjoyed the meal and your company even more."

She leaned toward him, and expected he'd give her a quick hug. She wanted that embrace so much her empty arms ached. But she asked him to leave. Instead of an embrace, he strode toward the door and didn't look back.

After the front door shut, she watched him out the window. Alyssa huddled with Josh on the two-flat's front steps, the same spot that she and Mrs. Syed chatted as the street traffic roared by. Whatever Pierce said caused her leap to her feet and pull a business card for her cake-baking business from her back pocket. She also grabbed a pen from Josh and scratched something on the back of the card. What was that about? Did he want to order a cake?

After climbing into the U-Haul truck, he looked back toward her window, shielding his eyes from the sunset. Even from where she stood, sadness clouded his gaze.

Pierce waved to her. And she waved goodbye. Forever.

~~~~~

The drive back to Shallow Stream seemed to take days rather than hours. Kendra had given up on them. He wouldn't. His short chat with Alyssa gave him the hope he needed. Kendra's best friend promised she'd help with the idea that burst inside of him out of nowhere.

He crossed the Shallow Stream border but didn't head back to the cottage. He couldn't see Aunt Meryl, even though she'd be thrilled to get the motorcycle unloaded and back home. As promised, Rob was waiting for him outside the barn.

Together, they dragged the motorcycle from the truck and maneuvered the bike down the ramp and into the empty barn.

"Thanks for the help," Pierce said. "How was your Canada trip?"

"Always good to be back home. As much as I enjoyed visiting with my parents, I thought about Jill and the girls the whole time."

After they situated the bike against a former horse stall in the unused barn, Robert tapped his shoulder and offered him a ride back from the truck rental place.

"I'm fine. I'll drive there and run the five miles home." That's what he needed, a full-out run that made his legs burn and let him think. "See you soon, and thanks."

Pierce drove past the high school toward downtown Shallow Stream. Cort and some other boys he didn't recognize raced around the track. Usually, he would've stopped and hopped out. Asked how their summer was going. Not this evening. When he approached Winston Avenue, where his apartment, now clean, waited for him, he drove right past to his destination. Cutting the truck's ignition and waving to the business' owner, he reached into the backseat for his running shoes. He turned in the keys and signed the required paperwork, and then he was out of there. After the first few strides, his muscles squeezed and his thoughts faded, all but one. How could he possibly let Kendra go, even if that was what she wanted?

His musings filled with his conversation with Alyssa. The idea had been spur of the moment, a way to finally welcome Kendra to the McFarland family. A combination welcome-to-the-family and birthday party for Kendra would surprise her. With Alyssa baking the birthday cake and him taking care of the food, Kendra would have a day she'd always remember.

Chapter Twenty-One

The following morning, Pierce sat on his cottage front porch. Jill and her daughters joined him.

"Whoa, this idea could backfire on you big time," his sister said. Yet, she smiled as she French braided Jocelyn's hair. "You're done." She patted her eldest daughter's head.

"Let's go inside." The last thing he needed was Aunt Meryl hearing prematurely about his idea. "Where's Rob?"

"Mowing the grass, his favorite activity here. Every Christmas he hopes to spot a riding mower tucked next to the Christmas tree."

Together, they gathered in the dining room of Pierce's cottage. The apple pie Jill baked that morning for Aunt Meryl and her friend Grace's planned visit scented the space. Cinnamon and apples made his stomach grumble.

Until Kendra arrived, his life had been a blur. Now, he could remember every detail of each moment they shared together. How Kendra's eyes shone right before she laughed. How she'd smooth back her curls whenever she wanted to think about what she'd say instead of blurting the words. How she bit her lip whenever she started to become nervous.

"I want a braid 'do too," Ava said. She raised her arms and Jill positioned her younger daughter into the dining room chair.

A few minutes later, Jill looked up as she braided her second daughter's hair. "David's death impacted us all more than we realized." After she completed her braiding, she headed into his kitchen to check the blueberry pie's progress.

Jocelyn frowned at the apple pie. "Two pies for two ladies?"

His sister squeaked open the oven door. "Don't even ask. Aunt Meryl couldn't remember if Grace liked blueberry or apple pie better. I thought I'd better make both."

Resetting the oven timer, she returned to the dining room table and resumed their conversation. "When Kendra stayed here, that grin of yours never left your face. I'd like to see it again. It's a great idea you thought up for the party for Kendra. What have you got to lose? Plus, her best friend supports you. You can't get a better endorsement than a best friend's stamp of approval."

Yes, he'd been surprised at how Alyssa endorsed his idea.

"She's not going to tell Kendra?" His sister pulled her own hair back into a high ponytail. The look, coupled with her thin build, made Jill appear to be the age of one of his high school students.

He had to believe Kendra's friend wanted the best for her. They deserved a chance. That was all this was, a final opportunity after Kendra sent him away, acting like she never wanted to see him again. "Alyssa promised she wouldn't say a word. I'm certain Kendra will ask what the two of us discussed. I'll let Alyssa handle that. I can trust her."

"We better start planning. With Kendra's birthday coming up, we don't have much time to make this right."

Pierce held up the yellow legal pad with his long to-do list. He had three days until the big day. "Alyssa said she'd call Kendra's other friends. I'll take care of the McFarlands. Kendra will finally get to meet us all, and I hope she sees we're not all bad. She'll get the big bash Aunt Meryl promised her, and more. I hope she enjoys parties. Alyssa claims she does, and even more, unlike me, Kendra loves surprises." He couldn't think of anything much worse than a surprise birthday party held in his honor.

What about Aunt Meryl? Jill asked, silently mouthing the words over Jocelyn's head so the girls wouldn't hear.

"She's family, so I'll invite her. She can decide if she wants to attend." That ache in his neck started up again as soon as he uttered his aunt's name. Aunt Meryl ranked as the last person Kendra wanted to see. If closure could occur, his aunt needed to attend.

"If Aunt Meryl attends, she can ride with me," Jill said. "That will take some of the pressure off you."

Pierce wanted to cover his ears over his delightful nieces singing an off-key version of some pop kid song again and again and again. "Thank you."

He had also invited Pastor Thomas, after they had several discussions that always concluded with prayers. In the end, Pierce decided to go it alone.

"How else can I help?" she asked.

"That's okay, I can—"

"Yes, big brother, you can." She lifted the yellow, lined legal pad that rested in the middle of the dining room table. "See that massive to-do list of yours that looks as long as a literary novel? I want to help. I like Kendra too. I'll root for both of you."

"Thanks." At least someone saw relationship potential. Too bad Kendra didn't fully agree.

He took a glance at his list that he had spent most of last night composing. Had he forgotten any details? Kendra deserved this birthday party, especially with her mom and dad both gone. He wanted every moment to be perfect. "I'll cook up vats of chili and bring onions, shredded cheese, and heaps of green salad. Alyssa volunteered to bake a red velvet birthday cake, Kendra's favorite. Want to make cornbread? Never mind." He shook his head, thinking of their biggest problem. "Bring Aunt Meryl, and you'll tackle the most difficult task."

"I have a great cornbread recipe, and I'll include a bowl with jalapeno peppers so I won't be tempted to make my spicy version. That's the only way to eat cornbread. I know not everyone agrees. I'll make a large fruit salad too," she said.

Twenty minutes later, the oven timer binged. His sister leapt to her feet again like the jack-in-the-box her daughter Ava loved so much. For now, the two girls who perched at the dining room table remained quiet as they again knitted. Even he could see that their doll scarves contained even stiches that would make Kendra smile.

What would Kendra say when all the McFarland family appeared together? He pictured the scene with a line trailing down her apartment stairs and spilling onto her side street. Mrs. Syed offered them the use of a large tent she had purchased for her daughter's wedding. Alyssa would take care of keeping Kendra busy and away from the two-flat building. It all started to come together. Kendra would get the welcome she had expected, plus the birthday party that would be a surprise. Then she would either wrap her arms around his neck to thank him or never speak to him again.

~~~~~

Kendra had to face facts, but she cringed each time she did. She'd asked Pierce, no, she *told* him not to call her or contact her. He had listened. What did she expect? Had she ever treated a guest with such rudeness? At first, she even forgot to offer him a glass of ice water after he and Josh loaded the truck with the motorcycle. Since when did she become so rattled she forgot to be a gracious hostess?

Every time she reached for her phone, she forced herself to get up and walk laps around her apartment so many times her arches ached. She'd only be disappointed that he hadn't reached out to her. After what she said about his aunt, she couldn't call him or blame his decision.

Even if his aunt forgave Kendra, the problem about David remained. That wouldn't change. Mrs. McFarland would never let loose of the idea that Kendra's phone call about being pregnant had upset David, and he walked, distracted, in front of that tour bus.

She settled in with her knitting, and she worked on the first of two afghans for the babies. The pastel green and white design soothed her; she hoped her little ones would curl up under the blankets someday.

She wouldn't think about it anymore. It remained out of her hands now.

Chapter Twenty-Two

In the late morning, Pierce's fingers itched to text or call Kendra. Twice he found himself reaching for his phone, never wanting to hear her voice more. But he had to keep his promise to leave her alone. She wanted that, not him. Besides, if he spoke to her, he might leak something about the party.

Taking another trip out to his Jeep, arms loaded with strings of lights that caught his hands like a net, Pierce wiped away the perspiration that dotted his forehead. At least the day of Kendra's party would be warm and sunny, without a single raincloud. Returning to his cottage, he loaded the last vat of chili, the silver pot handles slippery in his hands. He checked his to-do list that managed to grow longer overnight. Everything for the best chili ever cooked had been packed.

"Want to take the cornbread?" Jill asked.

"It won't fit." He glanced toward the farmhouse. "How's Aunt Meryl?"

"She refuses to go to the party. No surprise. Jocelyn is holding court in the farmhouse's living room and trying to persuade her now.

"You sent your five-year-old in to try to change Aunt Meryl's mind?"

"Remember how much you loved birthday parties when you were five? No one could be a better salesperson than our Jocey. She chatted about red velvet birthday cake, trick birthday candles, balloons galore, party games, presents wrapped with sparkly bows. I hope she's not too disappointed when she learns there won't be a clown who juggles, like at her friend's birthday party."

Although he couldn't juggle, the clown might turn out to be him. Kendra could kick him out the moment she saw him. She said no contact. Normally, he'd respect any woman's request for him to leave her alone. This seemed different. Meeting the whole family mattered to her more than anything. Still, he pictured her leaning over as she whispered in his ear, "Please leave, and this time, don't come back."

"You okay?" Jill asked. "I lost you there for a sec."

"Fine. Nervous about the party. I hope Alyssa's right that Kendra loves surprises. I don't. The McFarlands in one giant tent, that'll be a big shock." And it could be overwhelming, despite Kendra saying how much she wanted family. After all the hurt they created, she might not want the McFarland family.

"She's her best friend; she should know. Don't worry. What's the worst that can happen?"

Aunt Meryl could make a scene. Until recently, he never thought his aunt could behave with such disregard for others' feelings.

He wouldn't let himself think about what could be even worse. If the party didn't go well, it might be his final time to ever see Kendra. "I'm going to head out now to Milwaukee and go set up."

~~~~~

Once Pierce arrived at the Milwaukee two-flat, he spotted the backyard tent Josh had assembled. After he scrubbed the already-clean tables, he put out the bowls, plates, and silverware that clattered, not caring how much extra cleanup they'd cause. A warm breeze wafted through the tent. The "door" flapped. What if Kendra didn't like any of the McFarland family, in addition to his aunt? He started to list all of their idiosyncrasies. At McFarland gatherings, laughter pealed louder than the music. With one music teacher and a school orchestra leader in the group, singing, often off-key, to the chagrin of the teachers, would fill the space. No matter what, it would be a late afternoon and evening to remember.

Soon, relatives poured into the tent.

"Great to see you."

"How can we help?"

"We're meeting David's wife? Can't wait," several said. They'd also meet the woman he cherished, Pierce wanted to reply, but he forced himself to stay quiet.

Ten minutes before Kendra's planned arrival, Pierce began to quiet the crowd. Even relatives he hadn't remembered ever meeting joined the group of at least forty people, probably more. He pulled out every teacher trick, and even resorted to the "one, two, three, look at me," he learned during the unfortunate summer when he worked as a kindergarten camp counselor. It didn't impress the kindergartners and ranked as more of a disaster with the adults.

"Kendra will arrive any minute. Let's make this a surprise," he said. That worked.

"She's parking her car," Jill said. "Quiet everyone, please."

Pierce's heart pounded. Maybe he invited too many people, who now filled the tent. He glanced over to Jill, who gave him the thumbs up.

Then, the time came. Kendra approached the tent as she chatted with Alyssa. The two women chuckled, and his heart lurched. If he could, he'd bottle up the sound of Kendra's voice and laughter.

"What's going on?" Kendra asked outside the tent door. "Why is this tent here? I hope Mrs. Syed knows that someone borrowed her tent. This tent means a great deal to her. If something happened to it, she'd be heartbroken."

He smiled. Typical Kendra, she always thought of someone else first.

Across the tent, he spotted Kendra's landlord. Mrs. Syed covered her mouth to hold in her laughter.

One step more forward and she was in the doorway. The cry came in unison the way they'd practiced. "Surprise! Happy Birthday, Kendra. Welcome to the family."

She placed her hand on her neck as if she tried to catch her breath. Tears shimmered. "I...I don't know what to say. My first thought was why are you all here?"

His relatives laughed.

"For you," Alyssa said and wrapped her arm around Kendra.

Jill rushed to Kendra's side and handed her a tissue from her dress pocket. "We're celebrating you." She kissed Kendra's cheek. "We're so happy it's your birthday, and you're part of the family." His sister handed Kendra another tissue.

"Oh, oh. I am surprised." She shot a pretend-angry look at Alyssa. "I thought best friends told each other everything."

Then the moment he waited for happened. She looked around, confused by the fact that she only recognized a handful of the partygoers.

"Thank you, uh, everyone," she said. Her cheeks reddened when she spotted him. Kendra grabbed the edge of a folding chair to keep standing upright.

He sprinted forward. Pierce couldn't let her tumble. When she smiled so that her cheeks glowed beneath the tears, he hoped she'd keep smiling. "For the 'Welcome to the McFarland family' part of the celebration, you'll get to meet everyone." The party Aunt Meryl had promised and never provided.

Her face lit up like they'd given her the best possible gift. "Oh, now I fully understand. I guess I'm still in shock. How wonderful. Thank you, thank you all. I want to say hello to all of you. Hi, I'm Kendra."

Everyone laughed.

~~~~~

"I guess you knew my name already. I can't promise I'll remember all your names," she said. She placed her hand on her heart. Family, tons of them, and they congregated here to meet her. Kendra couldn't imagine a better birthday present. Thank goodness she kept her phone charged. She could take lots of pictures of the people she'd call family. Kendra blinked back happy tears.

"If you forget our names, you can peek at our nametags," Jill said.

"Thank you, whoever thought of that, and this surprise party is brilliant," Kendra said.

"Pierce thinks of everything," Jill added.

Everything, except he forgot to contact her while he planned her party during the past few days. When they weren't supposed to have any more contact with each other, how could she fault him? Besides, planning a party took a lot of time. He probably didn't want to give away his secret.

She hurried over to him, unable to stop her smile. Clutching his hand in hers, his strong touch made her nerve endings spark.

She gazed over her shoulder at all the party guests, then turned back to him. "I missed you so much," she whispered.

His dark eyes softened. "And I missed you. I'm glad you didn't turn around and stomp out of the tent."

"I'm sorry about my waterworks. They're all happy tears, I promise. Thank you for this. Did Alyssa tell you I love surprises?"

"She did." Hugging her, he peered behind her and spotted her best friend standing close by. "Thanks, Alyssa, for all of your help. We couldn't have pulled this off without you."

Alyssa stepped forward and joined them. "Kendra, aren't you going to meet all the family?"

"I'll introduce you to everyone, if you let me," Pierce said, his voice low.

The timbre of his deep voice sent a shiver up her arms. Those same arms that she wanted to fling around Pierce's neck and pull him in for a longer hug. Not with everyone watching, though. Kendra placed her hands behind her back and clasped them together to keep from embracing him.

"I'd love to meet your family. Is your aunt Meryl here?"

"Last I heard she's sitting in the car with the window open. I'll go check on her in a while. Jocelyn did an amazing job of convincing my aunt to attend. I hope she isn't disappointed that a mermaid won't be in attendance," he said, joking. "This party may not be up to a five-year-old's standards."

She nodded, but no longer could she smile. "I don't think sitting outside in this heat in a parked car counts as attending this party. In fact, it could be dangerous for her health. May I go talk to her? Thank her for traveling all this way for a party for me?" It would be difficult, but she really needed to speak to Mrs. McFarland and tackle the hurt feelings on both sides.

"You're the guest of honor," he reminded her. "Meet everyone first."

"Okay, let's start with the introductions, but I must go speak with her after you introduce me." She took a deep breath, and some of her childhood shyness resurfaced. "You could say something about each of them to help me better remember each one. I'm good with names."

"Let's start with my Uncle John. He teaches chorus and general music at the local middle school. You can remember him as the one scowling when the singing starts. He's been known to put his hands over his ears. Don't take it personally."

"Singing? I hope no one makes me sing. It isn't karaoke, is it?" Her stomach flipped. "I'm a tone-deaf singer. Promise, I'll clear the room. You'll have the shortest party ever."

He squeezed her shoulder, and she paused to remember his warm touch that snatched away her nervousness.

"You're in for quite a fun night," he said. "The guest of honor doesn't need to sing. Besides, we sing in groups and have the rest of the audience rank us. Uncle John's group always wins. He sings louder than everyone else to drown out the other singers. That's later."

When he finished the introductions, she couldn't wait any longer. Otherwise, she'd never venture outside to encourage Mrs. McFarland to attend the party. "Before you serve that delicious-smelling chili that causes my stomach to rumble with hunger, I'm leaving for a few minutes to speak to your aunt." She said the words with what she hoped equaled the same kindness and firmness when one of her library patrons had many overdue books.

He squeezed her hand. "Want me to go with you?"

Shaking her head, she meandered through the tent into the breeze that rivaled her hair dryer's heat. Her palms perspired as she strode into her two-flat's backyard. Rushing past Mrs. Syed's flower garden, the blooms' scents encouraged her calming breaths, one after another. With each step, her sundress fluttered. The uneven stone pathway led past the side of the apartment building and toward the parking lot. From a distance, she spotted Jill and Rob's silver SUV that glinted through the late-day sunshine. With the front car door flung open, Meryl McFarland scowled as she approached. The woman's lips thinned. Her eyes narrowed. For a moment, Kendra expected her to slam the car door. Lock the door despite the ninety-degree afternoon.

She paused. *Please God, give me the strength to say the right words.* "May I speak to you?" Kendra asked.

"I can't stop you." Perspiration moistened the woman's temples and dribbled onto her neck.

Kendra held out her hand, the same way Pierce had greeted her when she arrived that afternoon to shouts of "Surprise!" Unlike the first time she met Meryl, she didn't let her hand fall back to her side.

"I'd like you to join us for the meal of fresh green salad, cornbread, and chili complete with fixings of onions and shredded cheddar cheese." Her mouth watered at the thought of the meal.

"Why?"

She shuddered. Had this been a mistake? Would the woman reject her overtures once again? No, she wouldn't let that happen. Overhead, one, and then another airplane thundered.

"It's so loud here in Milwaukee. How can you stand living her?"

Kendra inched closer to the car. She spotted Meryl's tear tracks. Eyes rimmed with red. "I confess; I prefer Shallow Stream."

Meryl tilted her head.

She contemplated all the ways she could approach Mrs. McFarland. The dangers of sitting in a hot car wouldn't impress her. The woman deserved the truth, so Kendra spoke from her heart. "You're part of my family. Let's go inside and enjoy the food and the company. Together we'll bow our heads and thank God for our meal and for family blessings."

To Kendra's surprise, Meryl accepted her still outstretched hand.

"I don't trust you, and I haven't forgiven you." The woman's dark eyes gleamed in the same manner David's did when he hurled an insult.

She bit back her silent response of "For what?" Despite the even stance she learned from playing sports, her legs wobbled and her knees trembled.

Meryl jerked her chin toward the tent. "Guess I could join the others and eat a nibble."

"Everyone would like if you made that choice." The truth counted as a start. Kendra linked her arm with Meryl, who held her stiff forearm as far away as she could.

"Careful, I've tripped over these stones," Kendra said.

"Your landlord should replace them. A woman of my age could tumble and break a hip."

She grasped Meryl tighter. "I'll make sure that doesn't happen."

They trudged together through the yard. The walk back took triple the time as Kendra's rush to the apartment's parking lot. As soon as she flung the tent flap open, Pierce gave her a thumbs up.

"Time to eat, everyone. Let's let Kendra go first." More quietly, he added, "Please start off the food line. No one will eat until you do. Thank you for persuading my aunt to join the party. Uncle John will have her chuckling in no time."

Huddled between Uncle John and a woman with Meryl's fair skin and dark curls, Mrs. McFarland chatted. Once she even threw back her head. Her curls bounced as she belly-laughed.

Had Kendra ever seen her smile? A breath of relief filled her lungs. "I'll go ahead. Did you make all this food?"

She looked deep into his eyes, astounded. It seemed as though a cool breeze brushed her neck and nudged her closer to him. If only she could open her heart and rush into his open arms.

Hands on her shoulders, he pointed her toward the steaming vats of chili and her favorite comfort food, corn bread.

"I prepared the chili. Let me know if I need to season it more."

"I'm sure everything tastes perfect."

And her prediction came true.

Toward the end of the meal, during which she sat between Jill and Pierce, having Jocelyn and Ava taking turns sitting on her lap, he stood up.

"Uncle John, please plug in your karaoke machine."

During the next few hours of the singing performances, she chuckled each time Uncle John clasped his hands over his ears and grimaced.

She looked around and shook her head at all the party decorations and the planning that must have been required. The white tent contained rows of tables, and she couldn't help but think of a wedding reception. Her favorite sunflowers adorned each table. How did Pierce know that? She had never told him. Maybe Alyssa suggested the flowers? White lights like stars twinkled overhead.

"This is all so..." she began as she and Pierce joined Jill, Robert, Jocelyn and Ava for their turn to sing karaoke. "Wonderful, like every other birthday party rolled in together."

She fanned herself. "No one has ever treated me as well as you do." Could this even be real? He seemed too considerate, too kind. Maybe after her past experience, letting someone love her frightened her the most. When would the insults begin? His aunt excelled at barbs. If she opened up to Pierce, then he might start like David had done. She glanced at him as he chatted with his nieces, who he loved like his own kids. Love. Did she love Pierce?

So many names had been spoken, she couldn't possibly remember them all. After relatives introduced themselves, she finished her last spoonful of chili as cheddar cheese dribbled down her chin. Pierce dabbed her chin with a napkin, and she giggled.

"We're up for our song next. Once we finish our song, I'll stand right by your side, and I'll whisper the names if you forget," he said.

Her heart beat faster with him next to her. "I like that idea."

"So do I."

As the final family performance, Jocelyn and Ava took the lead and belted out "Jesus Loves Me." Uncle John gave their group a thumbs-up rather than a critique. Maybe the heartfelt words of faith overcame their lack of musical finesse.

At Pierce's urging, Kendra opened up the pile of birthday gifts. She sat in a chair in the middle of the tent while Alyssa jotted the gift givers' names for the thank you notes she planned to write the following day. "Thank you, Emmalynn, for the bamboo knitting needles. Thank you, Catherine and Teresa, for the merino wool yarn. What a luxury. I love the aquamarine color. How did you know?"

Her fingers ached as she ripped open packages. Each time she repeated the gift-giver's names and gave sincere thanks. She had to remember them all. Their generous presents caused her to need to pause more than once and take a deep breath. The mountain of wrapped gifts dwindled.

A half hour after she opened all the birthday presents, Pierce motioned to the guests. "Dessert is now being served." He handed Kendra a plate with the first piece of cake large enough to feed a family.

She took a bite of the cake, delighted as the creamy decadence tingled on her tongue. "This red velvet birthday cake that tastes so scrumptious, Alyssa baked. While the library we work at remains closed, my best friend started up her own baking business. We're fortunate she's taking new customers," Kendra said. "Thank you, everyone, for the best night of my life. You've made my dream of meeting the McFarland family come true." She glanced back to Pierce. "You don't know how much this perfect evening has touched my heart."

Chapter Twenty-Three

Two hours later, Kendra had spoken to every guest except one. With Pierce's help, recalling the names didn't overwhelm her.

"I'll give you a crash course on every tip I've learned about remembering student names," he told her.

More than once, she reached for his forearm and gave him a pat to reassure herself he stood at her side.

"Let's check in on your aunt."

Meryl sidestepped them and retreated to the tent's corner.

He frowned. "Maybe we can catch up with her later."

After their third effort to chat with his aunt, he didn't comment again.

At 9p.m., a few families with young children yawning in their arms bid her goodnight. Couples holding hands pulled out phones and provided their contact information.

"I'm including you on the McFarland family newsletter. Sign up for our private Facebook page, which includes a recipe exchange. I'm so glad we could meet you, and I can't remember when I had so much fun," one cousin said.

The overhead lights shimmered like God's stars that filled Kendra's heart with hope. It ranked as a perfect night. "My thanks to you, a thousand times over," she said to Pierce. "I met your family. I'd given up on that goal. They're great, by the way, even if they can't sing much better than I can."

An hour later, someone, probably Jill, she guessed, unplugged the white lights that had enchanted Kendra. Only a handful of guests remained. In the semi-darkness illuminated only by tabletop tea lights, the tent dimmed. Soft shadows emerged. One glance at Pierce made her breath quicken.

He chuckled; his laugh that always made her giggle cut through her musings.

"Although my nieces stole the show, you underestimated your singing ability," he said.

The song's words of Jesus' love had given her voice a boost. Warmth ballooned inside her.

She had so many questions. Her eyes adjusted to the darkness, and the surroundings didn't seem as dark. Kendra placed her hand in his.

Pierce edged closer. "Uncle John says he wants you on his karaoke team at all the family parties. You're a game changer."

Her heart let in the love that filled his eyes when he gazed at her.

"You've given me a glimpse of your family. What great people." Kendra looked away. Despite the delicious meal of his homemade chili, her stomach churned.

"Even my aunt?"

She had spotted Meryl helping Jill load up supplies about a half hour earlier, but then his aunt returned alone. Kendra tried not to shiver.

"Even her. I'm glad she agreed to come in out of the heat and see her relatives. Your kindness touched my heart. This night...I'll remember this party, this magical night forever," she said.

In the darkness, he pulled her close and brushed his lips against hers. Then the kiss deepened. She melted into his arms, his warmth, and his love. His lips caressed her neck, and she shivered as his mouth closed again on hers.

She pulled away from him. "Pierce, I don't know..."

"Don't think. I'm not pressing you into anything. I want to get to know you better. Give me a chance," he said. "Give us a chance."

~~~~~

With Kendra in his embrace, someone tapped him on the shoulder. "Pierce, I must speak to you," Aunt Meryl said.

He couldn't believe it, or maybe he could. Only his aunt would have the nerve to interrupt his first kiss with Kendra. "Now?"

"It's an emergency. Come with me."

What could his aunt want? To interrupt such a private moment took a lot of guts. This had better be a true emergency.

"I'll be right back," he said to Kendra.

His aunt directed him toward the sweet table. "Your little party ended. You've given her what she wants. The chance to meet the McFarland family."

"That's the big emergency?" He swallowed hard to keep the anger that percolated within him at bay. He left Kendra's embrace for this?

Aunt Meryl strode close to him. Her voice fell so low that it resembled a growl. "This is it. The absolute last time."

The last time for what?

She wagged her finger so close to his face it almost brushed his nose. His aunt kept her voice as low as a growl. "She tried to charm all of our relatives. I told her earlier that I don't trust her, and now that ranks as doubly true. If that Kendra Hester ever steps foot again on the McFarland farm, not only will she not be welcome, you also will not be welcome. My heart breaks as I think about the possibility of seeing her again. I will not allow that to happen. I've experienced enough sadness."

Dumbfounded, he leaned toward his aunt, and he hoped the action would make her lower her voice. "Yes, you've gone through a great deal. I'm sorry you experienced heartbreak. What does this have to do with Kendra? And you not seeing me? You can't mean that. She's done nothing bad to this family. Everyone loves her." That statement included him.

He imagined sitting home alone on Christmas day, staring at the tree's bright lights. Cooking a Thanksgiving turkey big enough for only himself. The scent of turkey, cornbread, and stuffing would fill his small apartment. Maybe his family would drop by later and see him. Even if he could convince Kendra to remain open to love, could he change his aunt's mind? No, she made that clear. Would he give up his family for Kendra?

Aunt Meryl's eyes shone in the moonlight that glimmered through the tent's windows. "Don't let her back into the farmhouse. Don't you dare see her ever again. It's over. She'll tear our family apart. Did I make myself clear?"

"If I don't follow your directions, then you'll disown me," he said. "You can't be serious."

~~~~~

Behind him, Kendra gasped. This couldn't be happening. She didn't know if she could keep her voice from breaking as she stared at Mrs. McFarland. Even in the shadows, she spotted the scowl.

"You won't see me again. Don't worry. Either of you. I'm not going to ruin your family in addition to the other horrible crimes, Mrs. McFarland, you claim I committed."

Mrs. McFarland whirled. "You eavesdropped on a private conversation. That's just like you. Always taking what isn't yours."

"This is *my* mistake? I don't think so. I won't apologize," Kendra said. "The conversation involved me, and I should've been a part of it. For your information, I said I was happy your property was worth a lot because of the way your son spoke about growing up, when he did say anything. It sounded like he had nothing, absolutely nothing. I'm relieved to hear you raised him in a family of all sorts of abundant riches. I wanted happy memories for him because after we married, he no longer acted content."

Pierce started to say something, but she waved him off. "You've given me the perfect night. Know I'll never forget you or tonight. Thank you. Do not contact me again, Pierce. Whatever we had, it's over for good." Thanks to Mrs. McFarland.

Spine straight, she left the tent and didn't look back. The few remaining partygoers had gathered outside in front of the illuminated flower garden as her landlady dispensed gardening tips.

"Goodbye, Uncle John," she managed to say with a smile on her way out. "I'm glad I had the opportunity to meet you." The first and last time she'd ever see or hear the music teacher with a voice to rival any professional singer.

"Thank you, Mrs. Syed. We'll chat tomorrow on the front step. It was kind of you to let them borrow your tent." How would she ever tell her landlord about the night's conclusion? Her neighbor would be so disappointed.

She returned to her apartment, slammed the front door, and didn't bother to turn on the lights. The darkness matched her mood. In the spare bedroom, she ran her hands across the second baby dresser Josh had assembled earlier that day. Maybe Josh and Alyssa would become the couple she had hoped she and Pierce would be. Sitting in the bedroom's rocking chair, Kendra closed her eyes, and let the black night seep inside. She clasped her hands together, dropped to her knees, and began to pray.

Chapter Twenty-Four

Pierce slammed his hands on the steering wheel. Other cars whooshed by him on the expressway. One honked, and he saw his speed crept at forty-five miles per hour. At the next exit, he pulled off. The streetlights twinkled, and Pierce recalled the lights in the tent for Kendra's party that Jill had strung. His sister had turned a simple tent into a piece of art. None of it mattered if Kendra would never see him again.

In the night sky, he couldn't spot a single star. Even worse, he couldn't stop replaying Kendra's words. "I'll never forget you." The pain settled in his chest. It grabbed him and wouldn't let go. Parked on the side of the gravel road, he turned off the Jeep's ignition. Sweat beaded his forehead and slithered down his neck. He couldn't drive, not as he gasped for each breath that his lungs squeezed.

Hours later, his tires crackled across the driveway. He spied Aunt Meryl's silhouette etched in the kitchen window of the farmhouse. She waited up for him. No doubt she stored up more complaints about Kendra. He wasn't sure that his patience, tested over and over again, could endure another argument. Had the hour been earlier, he would've contacted Pastor Thomas. This time if his aunt pushed, he'd push back harder. He didn't know what scraps remained of their tattered relationship.

When he entered the farmhouse's kitchen, the scent of banana bread greeted him. He spotted his aunt standing next to the oven.

"You're home late," she said. "It's almost one in the morning. I worried about you."

"Don't." His aunt sounded like she had when he watched over David and his cousin kept him out late on weekends. The tone put his teeth on edge. "I'm an adult, and I can take care of myself."

She pulled the banana bread from the oven, then removed her oven mitts. "Thank you for inviting me to the party, Kendra's birthday party."

He raised his eyebrows. His aunt must have assumed if she baked his favorite treat, it would erase his memory about how the evening ended. "And also the 'welcome to the McFarland family.' You forgot that." Even in the dimness of the single kitchen light, her eyes lost some of their sheen. After she heard what he had to say, she'd burst. But he wouldn't back down, no matter what her reaction. He'd already lost any chance with Kendra.

"You can claim you will disown me, Aunt Meryl, but I have a right to be part of this family. So does Kendra. Whether you like it or not, I'll still attend family events. If Kendra will forgive me, I'll bring her to these events too. You can ignore me. But I'll be there. You did everything you could to make Kendra miserable. You won't accomplish the same thing with me. Don't try."

His aunt nodded and perched on the edge of the kitchen chair. Her shoulders sagged.

"I wouldn't have left Rob and Jill's SUV if it weren't for Kendra. I planned to swelter in that vehicle and throw my own private pity party. I looked forward to having everyone inside that tent worry and feel sorry for me."

Pierce said nothing. If his aunt wanted pity, she wouldn't get it from him.

"Ever since the party ended and I achieved my goal of breaking up you and Kendra, I've thought my actions might cause me to lose my family. I may throw away what Kendra so desperately wanted. I am so sorry. I had no right to try to dictate your life."

The ache in his chest simmered. Still, Pierce hugged his aunt, seeing another glimmer of her previous self. Would it last? She might've only said the words that he wanted to hear. Everything could remain the same.

"I'm not done," she said, raising her hand. "Don't think you can quiet me with your hugs. I admit Kendra has had a good influence on you during her short visit. I'm still not sold she's the right one for you, but I might change my mind over time. Until then, I'll try to keep quiet about your relationship."

Now that surprised him. His aunt even complimented Kendra, sort of.

"You deserve happiness, and I'm afraid I've been holding you back," she added.

"No, Aunt Meryl—"

"Yes," she interrupted. "I received an offer on the farm. Grace told me about a townhouse in her complex that's for sale. I'll look at it tomorrow with Joel Martin. If all goes well, I will buy it."

Pierce pulled up the kitchen chair next to her. "That's a little drastic. If you're worried about Kendra..."

"This has nothing to do with her. I've overstayed my welcome on this farm, and I tried to get it to still work in memory of your uncle. Without the goats, chickens, and horses that are too difficult for me to tend, the place no longer brings me joy. I don't think he'd want me to stay here, either. Grace said the townhouse has a small, fenced yard with a swing set that includes a brand new slide." She paused, and for the first time, she smiled. "I believe the house will perfect for my two great-nieces to come over and play. If, after my rude treatment of them during their time here, they'll still visit."

"It's your choice." Relief flooded him like the lake he hoped he and Kendra would visit someday.

"Could you come by the house after you get yourself unpacked? I think this sale offer is a good one, but I value your input. I know it's late and I shouldn't ask, but I won't be able to sleep until I've received your input about the sale."

"No worries." Despite it being two in the morning, an hour later he had read over the contract three times. "Not a good deal, a great deal." His aunt wouldn't need to worry about money. For the first time in years, he didn't need to be concerned with her welfare. Although he wouldn't leave Jill stranded, seeing her great-nieces and helping out with babysitting would bring back his aunt's smile.

"You want to sell this place and move now? The farm has been your life, your home, for many years." He studied her, waiting for any sharp edges that conflicted with her determined words. He looked into his aunt's eyes, once again brighter.

"Yes, especially now. I'm ready to move on. Start something new. It took me a while, that's all." His aunt brought out the kitchen plates and placed them on the pressed tablecloth. Just-picked tulips decorated the table. The scent of his favorite banana bread sprinkled the air. "When you didn't come home, I baked for you. I think it's time I did something for someone else. Get involved in church again. Time for a change for the better."

As he reached for a piece of banana bread, Pierce could only hope his aunt told the truth. Still, it all came too late for him and Kendra.

Chapter Twenty-Five

Summer break for Pierce always moved at a speed that overshot every other season. August heat and humidity arrived with the start of a new school year less than a week away. More important, Kendra hadn't contacted him. Despite their agreement, he'd have to be the one to get in touch with her. If she didn't want to speak to him, at least he'd hear her voice one last time.

He pulled off his running shoes, and he checked his email for any updates on his employment applications to Milwaukee schools. He'd tried applying for every last-minute job opportunity that might arise: high school guidance counselor, English teacher, and middle school assistant principal. He'd give up his tenure, rescind his contract agreement, and even say goodbye to the town of Shallow Stream for another chance with Kendra, if she'd let him. If she wouldn't come to him, he'd go to her.

"Knock, knock," Jill called from the porch.

After he opened his cottage's front door, he studied his sister. "Come in. You look different."

She smoothed her hair and frowned. "How?"

"You don't have two little girls hanging on each arm, making you look like a scarecrow."

She gestured toward the farmhouse. "Aunt Meryl offered to watch them. She's cooking lasagna rollups using my recipe. Surprise, surprise." She flicked her dark hair over her shoulder. "She thinks I'm out clothes shopping. But I wanted to see you. Find out how you're doing."

"Check on the jilted boyfriend?" He cringed and stared out the front hall window. Had he ever been Kendra's boyfriend? The "jilted" part stung like an open wound.

His sister reclined next to him on the sitting room's gray loveseat. She curled her long legs beneath her, the way she had sat her entire life. His shoulders ached as he tried to forget how he and Kendra lounged here on that same loveseat not that long ago.

"What happened?" she asked. "Ready to talk?"

No, but maybe he should tell someone. He laced his running shoes, ready for his usual escape. He'd have to face the truth sometime.

"Everything seemed perfect at her party," she added.

Not until the end of the night did their relationship crumble into pieces so sharp, he didn't know if he could pull everything together again.

"Kendra had seemed thrilled to meet all of the McFarlands. She certainly won over Uncle John's heart. Then Aunt Meryl interrupted and had her say with every word soaked with venom. Kendra said she'd never be part of this family. I'm not supposed to contact her." So far, he'd honored Kendra's request, even as the thought of it made his whole body ache worse than his hardest run.

"Maybe Kendra doesn't want you to leave her alone."

He paused, and he pictured Kendra at his side. "I wanted a serious, loving relationship. I thought about marriage. Imagined Kendra here in this cottage, with us as husband and wife with the twins." Then he messed it all up. He had too much at stake not to try full throttle to win Kendra back.

His sister glanced at his laptop that stood open on the desk table in the room's corner. She viewed his most recent job application.

"Whoa. You'd really leave this town? You love Shallow Stream."

"That's all I ever thought I wanted — to live in Shallow Stream, work at Washington High School. First, I made sure David stayed okay throughout high school. Later, I took care of Aunt Meryl. It gave me purpose. With Pastor Thomas's help, I understand God gives me His purpose."

Jill nodded.

"To live here, work here, maybe even become a husband someday, that's my dream." The fact hurt more than a pulled muscle after a long run. If Kendra wasn't part of his life in Shallow Stream, he could live and feel empty anywhere.

He imagined the first day back at the high school with the students. When the students tumbled through the main school entrance and buzzed with excitement. Now, all he could think about was facing that day alone without Kendra. Without sharing the excitement of the new clubs and the students' reunion chatter whirring through the high school's hallways.

"Wonder how her pregnancy is going?" The back of his neck throbbed. Kendra and the babies had to be okay. But he'd never know if he didn't find out. He reached for his phone from his back pocket and fired off the text.

Hi Kendra,
I've been thinking about you, and I hope all is going well. Can we talk?

Not even a minute later, her return text flashed across the screen.

I'm in Shallow Stream this afternoon. I had business to take care of. Meet at Dimorio's in fifteen?

"Pierce?" his sister asked.

His fingers flew to answer Kendra's text.

"Got to go. See you later." He kissed the top of his sister's head, once, twice, three times. "Wish me the best. I'm off to see Kendra and make everything right." He rushed through the sitting room, kitchen and dining rooms to the bedroom. Once there, he yanked open the top dresser drawer. Pulling out the black velvet box he had purchased the morning of Kendra's party, he placed it into his pants' pocket.

Jill's footfalls followed him. "You're going to win her back?" she asked, her eyes wide.

"That's my plan. We're meeting at Dimorio's." He grabbed his Jeep's keys. Never had he sprinted from his cottage faster. "Pray for me. I'll do anything to get Kendra back in my life," Pierce called back over his shoulder as the cottage door slammed behind him.

He couldn't drive to Dimorio's fast enough, but he also didn't want to get pulled over for speeding. That was all he'd need. He couldn't delay seeing Kendra one second longer. Arriving in the restaurant's parking lot, he squeezed the steering wheel. Of all times, every parking space had been taken. After placing his Jeep a block away, he rushed to the restaurant. His chest ached from the adrenalin that fueled the sprint. Pierce had something to say to her, something she needed to hear.

Once at the Dimorio's threshold, he spotted the top of Kendra's head, her curls shining as she sat at the table they had once shared. If he had anything to say, those moments would continue.

"Hiya, Mr. McFarland," Cort called, standing near the cash register with a pile of menus in one hand.

Not now. Pierce couldn't keep Kendra waiting. "You work here now?" He prided himself on always taking time to acknowledge and speak to students wherever he met them. Never did he want them to believe they didn't matter, especially Cort. Still, his gaze drifted to Kendra. Focus.

"Yep, I'm the host here," Cort said, with a wide smile. "I've got the perfect table for you. It's in a quiet corner, but the sunlight sort of drifts in. Not too close to the kitchen noise or too breezy by the front door. It's the table we reserve for celebrities, if anyone famous ever strolled through the door, which hasn't happened yet. It could happen. We're all still hoping. Anyway, no one will bother you."

"Thanks, but I see someone I know. Did you have a good summer?" Pierce forced himself to chat.

"Yeah," his student said. "My mom's counting the days until the four of us are back in school. I'll miss the freedom. What about you, Mr. McFarland?"

Surprised, Pierce looked back at his always too-casual student. Cort never called him Mr. McFarland, even after Pierce's numerous requests. "I hope I'll remember it as the best summer ever."

He hurried past Cort, past the endless row of tables. When did this restaurant become massive? He rushed past the pizza-scented kitchen and toward the woman he pondered every day since that fateful night.

"Kendra." Saying her name aloud tasted more delicious than the pizza he hoped they'd share.

"Pierce, hi, it's so good to see you." She glanced past his shoulder. A frown morphed into a tentative smile.

"Mrs. McFarland. Hi, how are you?"

Why was his aunt here? Had she followed him? This wasn't a part of his plan. "Aunt Meryl, what are you doing here?"

She bit her lip and looked Kendra in the eyes. "I'm not here to cause trouble. I'm here to apologize and tell you the truth. I did invite you to visit, then decided at the time I couldn't face you. I acted like a coward, and I would handle it differently now. "

"Thank you. How did you know we were here?" Kendra asked.

She lowered her voice. "Grace saw you in town, and she told me. When I went to the cottage to see if Pierce knew where I could find you, Jill told me to come here." She studied the ground. "I wanted to give you this envelope right now in case you refused to ever see me again."

Ever since their discussion after Kendra's birthday party, his aunt seemed to keep her promise about not interfering. Facing Kendra in-person for the first time could spark all of her past anger.

"Please, sit down. Join us," Kendra said.

At least one of them remembered good manners. Still, this could not be good, Kendra and his aunt together again.

"Let's do this some other time," he said. "We can meet back at the house. I need to talk to Kendra. Alone."

His aunt had to take the hint.

Instead, she shook her head. "Thank you, Kendra, for the kind invitation. I'll only stay a minute, but I hope some time soon, we can get together and enjoy a home-cooked meal at my new place. I'll do the cooking." She glanced at Pierce before looking back to Kendra. "I'm cooking a lot and even baking now. I enjoy it again."

"That's great," Kendra said. "I bet you are a wonderful cook. You could teach me how to cook your favorite meals."

Aunt Meryl looked over her shoulder, then turned back to Kendra. "We'll whip up my famous beef bourguignon, and I'll disclose my top-secret ingredients."

A softness spread across Kendra's face. "I'd love if we could cook together."

Meryl leaned forward. "I found something that's yours. I discovered it in the motorcycle's glove box." She lowered her voice to a whisper. "I didn't open the envelope because it is addressed to you. But Pierce told me my son left you money hidden somewhere in the house."

Kendra shifted and accepted the thick envelope. "It's from David. I recognize his handwriting."

"I'll go now." His aunt edged away from the table.

"Please stay, at least to find out if it's what I think it may be." She scanned the note and pulled out a wad of cash deeper that the breadbasket that she positioned in front of the envelope to block anyone else's view. "Thank you for finding this. Do you need any money for your new place? I must use most of this for the twins' expenses and college fund, but I won't need all this money Please take whatever would help you."

Tears clouded his aunt's eyes. As Pierce touched Meryl's forearm, she grabbed the booth's edge. "You would do that for me, wouldn't you? Even after I called you a gold digger. You'd help me."

Kendra pushed the envelope toward her. "Of course. David was your son, and soon I'll have his babies. We'll always be connected. We're family."

A single tear dribbled down his aunt's cheek. "I'm proud to call you family. Thank you, but I don't need anything. I'm so sorry for my cruel treatment of you. Please give me another chance."

Pierce held his breath.

"It was challenging, but we can start over," Kendra said. "After all, you'll be the twins' grandma."

"Bless you. I'll leave you two alone. I wish you both the best."

If he hadn't witnessed the situation first-hand, Pierce would've never believed what had just happened.

Kendra half-stood and wrapped his aunt into a hug. For the first time, she looked pregnant and also truly happy.

His aunt strode from the restaurant, her shoulders back and her head held high for the first time since her son's death. Still, an ache settled in his shoulders and caused his neck to throb. Kendra needed closure, so she had contacted him. Wanted to see him again. Now, she had the money David wanted her to use for the future. This would be the last time Pierce would see her. Even his aunt would crowd together with her over the stovetop as she and Kendra cooked gourmet meals. She'd see Kendra and the babies more than he would.

"Sorry about my aunt's interruption."

"I welcomed the chance to talk to her again. How brave of her to apologize. She looks content, which warms my heart. I believe your aunt and I can have a positive relationship. It may take time."

He scrubbed a hand down his face. A second opportunity to make things right transpired for Kendra and his aunt. Could he convince Kendra to give their relationship another chance? He pictured the future scene. The twins would crawl, then toddle through the cottage. The smells of bubble bath and lavender baby lotion would scent the bathroom. He'd expand the kitchen and turn the sitting room into a playroom. Floor-to-ceiling windows would allow the morning sun to stream inside. Another bedroom or two added would transform the cottage into a family home. Shrieks and giggles from the twins would wake him and Kendra each morning. Kendra's knitting tucked next to the bed they'd share together, holding each other throughout the night as husband and wife.

He cleared his throat. "You look healthy." Her beauty made him hold in a gasp. "How's the pregnancy?"

"I couldn't feel better. I'll start seeing Dr. Engel more often soon."

He settled across from her into the booth, hoping to stretch out their time together. "That's great. Josh told me he helped you with things you needed around your apartment." Pierce could've assisted, too, had he been asked. He ignored the gut punch and imagined Josh assembling the second crib instead of him. As fast as he could've driven to Milwaukee, he would've dropped everything else and arrived at her apartment.

The waiter brought by a heaping salad for both of them. "What pizza do you want to order? My treat," she said. "It's about time, right?"

He pushed away his salad. They needed to talk. Decide their relationship once and for all. Like him, she had to recognize how great they'd be together.

"I'm happy to help you." The booth's table between them seemed to stretch on as far as Lake Michigan. "If it's finding a bigger apartment or researching pediatricians for the twins. Whatever you need," he said.

She chuckled. "I knew you'd say that, which was why I couldn't talk to you during the last few months. You always want to assist, which I appreciate. I needed to also know I could be independent and overcome all the obstacles I faced."

He shouldn't have expected anything. They had already said goodbye on that perfect night that turned into a disaster. Seeing her again and knowing this really would be the last time ranked as the worst possible torture. His shoulders slumped.

"Lots happened since I last saw you." She took a deep breath.

If Kendra could forgive his aunt, she could possibly forgive him too.

She took a deep breath. Kendra discreetly counted the hundred-dollar bills before slipping the windfall back into the manila envelope. "While the money will be for the twins, I'm also giving a donation to a program that helps women and men who've been in emotionally abusive relationships."

"Strange as it sounds, David would've approved." Still, the fact she had to endure those insults from the person who should've treasured each moment with her brought back his shoulder ache.

"There's more." She paused and took a sip of water. "I'm moving."

His heart lurched. Moving, where? No. This couldn't happen. He forced himself to stay seated in the red vinyl booth that captured him like a prison cell. They needed time together, not to live farther apart. His throat ached. This meant a true goodbye. He couldn't let it happen. With love to shower her, he needed time to show her his feelings.

She had to at least hear the truth before she made her move away from him.

"I can't enjoy life without you. These months away from you have been miserable and lonely," he said.

"For me too."

Pierce took a deep breath. Was there hope?

She smoothed a stray curl. "I've been to Shallow Stream three times in the last two weeks."

Yet, she had never contacted him.

"The library director offered me that part-time circulation supervisor job. Remember? Meg and I have been selling our knitting projects online. We're doing okay."

He wanted to offer her congratulations, but one thing she said trumped everything else. Pierce had to make sure he heard her right. "You're moving here? You'll live in Shallow Stream?"

"Yes. We'll be in the same town. I know you like to visit the library. We're sure to run into each other. I didn't want it to be awkward. If you don't want me to move here, I'll live in another town close by."

Gulping the ice water in front of him, the coolness soothed his throat like Kendra's upcoming move gave him hope.

She leaned closer, and her curls tumbled across his forearm, leaving behind a trail of goose bumps. He wanted to jump from the booth and gather her in his arms. But he had to respect the promise he made when they parted.

"This time apart let me think. I'm willing to open up my heart to you, if you'll give me another chance," she said.

"I want you to give *me* a second chance. You won't regret it." He stood up. "I'd love it if you'd move back here, because Kendra, I love you."

Someone standing behind him cleared his throat.

"Sorry, Mr. McFarland. Just checking to make sure you had the best dining experience ever at Dimorio's. We appreciate online reviews, especially five-star ones. I guess you are having that great summer you wanted. I don't think you need luck."

Not exactly the romantic way he expected to proclaim his first "I love you" to Kendra. At least Cort hadn't whipped out his phone and videotaped the whole thing, sharing their moment with the high school and all of Shallow Stream.

"Thanks, but it would be a perfect dining experience with some privacy," Pierce said.

"Oops, I get the hint. Catch you later," his student said.

Kendra burst out laughing, the sound he'd waited two months to hear.

After he glanced over his shoulder to make sure Cort hadn't eavesdropped, he touched her hand, marveling at her skin's softness. He never wanted to forget how her hand fit into his.

~~~~~

Pierce's words warmed her more than that smoldering June afternoon they'd met. She blinked back the happy tears that threatened to trickle down her cheeks. "I love you too. That's why I wanted to move back, to be close to you and the McFarland family. I hope your aunt's new home will be nearby." She never thought she'd say those words, but she meant them. She took a deep breath. "Could I rent out your cottage?" She couldn't possibly even dream that they'd be together in the bungalow as a family someday.

He scooted into the seat next to her, close enough that she could smell his woodsy cologne. The booth's vinyl made a large pucker sound that, to everyone in the restaurant, sounded like the biggest smooch ever. Kendra laughed so hard, happy tears again filled her eyes.

Leaning in, Pierce took her in his arms, and his strength in the embrace buoyed her. He wrapped a single curl in his fingers. Tilting her chin, she looked into his eyes, the eyes she wanted to peer into forever. His lips brushed against hers and made her shudder. With his hand cupped against her throat, he kissed her, and, uninterrupted this time, she melted into his embrace.

Then, Pierce dropped to one knee at the edge of the booth.

Her breath caught.

In the newly quieted restaurant, her heart thudded, ready to burst. She never let her gaze go anywhere but his eyes.

As he fell to one knee, his fingers brushed against the velvet box he stowed away earlier. He pulled the box from his pocket and opened it for her to see the diamond ring.

"I love you, Kendra Faith Hester. Please keep the McFarland name. Let me love you and these babies forever. Will you marry me?"

Wrapping her arms around his neck, she pulled him close and breathed in his delicious scent that made her want to never leave his embrace. With a single word, she could be part of Pierce's life each day. What could possibly be better? "Yes, I'll marry you," she said, kissing him back.

"When you're ready. You pick the date. No pressure," he said. "All I ask is that we get married in the church. I've been spending a lot of time there, and it would mean a lot to me to have Pastor Thomas officiate."

"Me too." Surrounded by family and friends, a church wedding would take place with the man she loved. She blinked back the tears of joy.

This afternoon, tomorrow, would that be too soon? Still, they didn't need to rush. Their love would endure.

In the aisle next to the booth, she hugged him, careful not to crowd the babies. He placed his other hand on her belly. The babies remained part of this too. One of the twins kicked. The other rolled with new vigor. "I'll take that as a rousing yes from the babies too," she said, giving her belly a gentle pat.

Around them, the restaurant patrons burst into applause.

"Kendra Hester McFarland, welcome to the family we'll build together. Nothing could make me happier or be more right."

Family. With Pierce at her side loving her, Kendra couldn't wait to start their life together, a life filled with love, faith, and family.

The End

The End

Finding Her Family's Love **Discussion Questions**

1. Kendra visited Shallow Stream to share her pregnancy news with the McFarland family. Yet, Pierce urged her to postpone revealing her news to his aunt. Do you agree with Pierce's motivation to protect his aunt? Should Pierce have asked Kendra to wait, and should Kendra have complied with his request?

2. Kendra kept her emotional abuse a secret. What other options did she have? How did the emotional abuse impact her throughout the story?

3. At one time in his life, Pierce relished his strong faith. What happened that weakened his faith? Have you ever experienced a time when your faith faltered? What did you do to restore your faith?

4. Forgiveness is one theme in the story. What additional themes appeared within the book that resonated with you?

5. Pierce loved Shallow Stream, Illinois, enough to give up a higher-paying teaching job in Chicago to return to his hometown. What qualities of Shallow Stream did Kendra enjoy? Would you like living in a town like Shallow Stream? If you could reside anywhere, what sort of place would you choose to live?

6. Meryl McFarland's relationship with her son David included misbeliefs. Have you ever been in a situation in which you held onto falsehoods regarding another person's actions and character? How did you accept the truth, and did it change the relationship?

7. Jill and Pierce remained close as siblings. What factors in their lives encouraged this strong relationship?

8. What sort of parents do you envision Pierce and Kendra will be?

9. If you could select one character from this story to have a heart-to-heart talk, which character would you pick? What advice would you provide?

About the Author:

Kayla Kensington and her family reside in the Chicago area. When not writing, she works as a librarian matching books to middle school readers. In addition, she teaches writing classes and shows young writers the power of words. She earned her MFA in writing from Lindenwood University.

Readers can find Kayla Kensington online:
kaylakensington.wordpress.com
Instagram: *@kayla_kensington*
kensingtonkayla@gmail.com